*A
Harlequin
Romance*

OTHER
Harlequin Romances
by JOYCE DINGWELL

Many of these titles are available at your local bookseller, or through the Harlequin Reader Service.

For a free catalogue listing all available Harlequin Romances, send your name and address to:

HARLEQUIN READER SERVICE,
M.P.O. Box 707, Niagara Falls, N.Y. 14302
Canadian address: Stratford, Ontario, Canada.

or use order coupon at back of book.

THERE WERE THREE PRINCES

by

JOYCE DINGWELL

HARLEQUIN BOOKS   TORONTO
                      WINNIPEG

Original hard cover edition published in 1972
by Mills & Boon Limited.

© Joyce Dingwell 1972

SBN 373-01808-8

Harlequin edition published August 1974

Printed in Canada

1808

CHAPTER I

... "ONCE upon a time there were three princes, a gracious prince, a charming prince, and a prince who was in-between."

Verity smiled nostalgically to herself as the old fairytale came back down the years to her. What favourite book of hers, or Robin's, had it been in? Not Hans Andersen, she knew. Certainly not Grimm.

She put the thought aside to listen attentively to Mrs. Prince who had prompted the childhood memory with her recounting of her trio of sons.

"Matthew is a wonderful person," she had told Verity, "Peter is a fascinating fellow, and Bart –"

"Yes, Mrs. Prince?"

"Is just Bart," his mother had related.

"Bart comes in the middle?"

"Matthew was our first, Bartley our second and Peter was our baby. Though none of them are babies now." Mrs. Prince had laughed ruefully. "In fact well into that stage of life when they should be providing me with grandbabies. If you can see your way to fall in love with any of them and marry him while I'm away, Miss Tyler, I'll be very pleased indeed."

"Do you say that to all your employees?" Verity had laughed.

"Only you and Priscilla. Oh, no, I'm a very discerning person." She had smiled warmly on Verity, and Verity who had liked her at once had smiled back.

"Priscilla is your secretary?"

"The firm's secretary for some years now. I don't know what holds up Bart."

"Then it's Bart and Priscilla?" As Mrs. Prince had broached the subject, Verity did not mind adding her bit to the cosy chat.

"Not officially, as I just said." Mrs. Prince had glanced down at the references that Verity had given her. "They do seem very promising," she praised ... then she had paused. "There is just one thing –"

"Yes, Mrs. Prince?"

"Do you think you'll stay on with us, or is this just a temporary fill-in for you? Oh, I'm sorry, my dear, and you don't have to answer, but so many of you English girls come to Australia just to look around. Not that I blame you, but –"

"You mightn't want me to stop after you've sampled me," Verity had laughed back. Then seriously she had promised: "I will stay." For she had to stay. *Now.*

It hadn't been the money, though certainly her fare out from England had depleted her savings, it had been her half-brother Robin. Robin was her junior, and the sole inheritor of her step-father's very comfortable estate ... at least it had been that. A slight biting of Verity's bottom lip. For so long as he had been grown up, Robin had fallen in and out of affairs, from everywhere his restless feet had taken him he had written back to Verity that he was in love. He was reckless, scatterbrained, completely irresponsible, but endearingly vulnerable – anyway, Verity found him that. Possibly, she conceded, she felt like this since he had been so delicate as an infant. Her mother, seeing the adoration her young daughter of her first marriage had had for the baby of her second marriage, had declared him Verity's child.

There were only four years between them, but Robin had

used those years abominably, Verity often thought ruefully, with his calls and demands, his S.O.S.'s for help. Mature beside his immaturity, she had been at his beck and call.

But it had been when he had written to England that he would need her no longer, that Adele would take over the "child" now, that Verity had made the longest journey of all. She had come from England to Australia to see Adele, assess her, because if Adele was marrying Robin with that inheritance in view, that comfortable estate that was to eventuate in several years' time on his twenty-fifth birthday, she had to tell her that circumstances had suddenly altered, that the Ramsay assets had dwindled, that Robin no longer was the favourable proposition he had previously been. It was interference, she was aware of that, but she was painfully aware, too, of the type of girl Robin had previously selected.

Of course, she had known intrinsically, if she had looked at Adele and seen love there, she would not have spoken, because it would not have mattered, love needs no reward. And as it had happened she had not spoken. But not because of any love, that had been apparent, but because Robin was not going to live long enough for any words to be needed to be said.

"A few months," the doctor had told Verity sympathetically when she had gone to him after one of Robin's frightening attacks that had occurred soon after her arrival. "But you would have suspected that, of course."

"Well, he was a delicate child."

"You knew him even then?"

"I'm his sister . . . at least a half-sister."

"I'm sorry – I thought you were his wife."

No, Adele was his wife. By the time Verity had arrived in Sydney, the girl had seen to that. She had also seen to it that Verity knew what she now intended.

"I have been in touch with a solicitor," she had said quite

7

coolly, "and he has told me that even if Robin doesn't reach the prescribed age, which by the way he seems to be going could happen, the money still comes to me."

What money? Verity had thought.

She had not told the girl, though, for she had known that she must keep her by Robin's side. Either this last love was a true love or Robin was too tired to change, but this time his infatuation was persisting. Verity had not dared risk Adele leaving her brother because of what that shock could mean. Because her own money was gone and she must refurbish it, because if by some means Adele found out the truth and left Robin she had to be here to pick up the pieces, finally but tellingly because she simply loved him for the little vulnerable boy he had been, she had refused to listen to Adele's pointed suggestions that she return to England . . . Robin's suggestions, too, when Adele prompted him, because Robin was pitifully weak.

"If you're waiting for a hand-out –" Adele had said baldly.

"I have a wife now, Verity," Robin had hinted more kindly.

But she had still remained. And she would remain. She *must*.

"I'll be staying, Mrs. Prince," she repeated. Repeated it definitely.

The business was a superior antique and furnishing business in a very superior Sydney suburb. Verity had worked in such a business in Chelsea, but the moment she had crossed the threshold of "Woman's Castle", she had known that this was an even more encompassing concern. The displays were beautiful, everything was elegant, in perfect taste.

"The woman in this Woman's Castle," she had praised Mrs. Prince, for that was the establishment's name, "knows what goes to make a home." She had quoted: "A home is a woman's castle."

"Only," Mrs. Prince had smiled, "it's a man."

"One of the three sons?"

"Originally my husband, he had the unerring touch. I'm afraid" ... ruefully ... "all I know is not to match pink and yellow. Oh, I got by after Grant died, and the boys were still young, but only with the help of his books and sketches. Then Bart took over."

"Then he is the inspiration?" For, Verity thought, looking around again, inspiration was the only word.

"Well ... at present."

"Only at present?"

"Bart always considers it strictly that."

"He doesn't want the business?"

"Bart," said Mrs. Prince unhappily, "just wants his health."

"Oh, I'm sorry. I mean I didn't want to intrude."

"You're not intruding, and anyway, you'll see."

"See?" she queried.

"Bart suffered an accident. He was badly injured. He has undergone several superficial operations, and he faces the real thing now." A troubled sigh. "When he agrees."

"Will there be complete recovery?'

"We hope so, and Matthew is very confident." Before Verity could ask, Mrs. Prince had explained, "Matthew is my doctor son. He's the eldest."

The mother had sat silent for a while, and Verity had not liked to break in on her thoughts.

"Perhaps Bart would have been, too," she had shrugged at length, "if it hadn't happened. I mean, there was that time lapse in his medical studies, and a man loses his enthusiasm."

"And Peter? Your youngest? Medically inclined as well?"

"Oh, no, though doubtless he could have skated through.

9

Everything comes much too easy to our Peter. Just now he's a dabbler, in anything and everything, profitably dabbling, or he wouldn't do it. Well, there are my three sons."

"But only the in-between concerned with Woman's Castle."

... "Once upon a time there were three princes, a gracious prince, a charming prince, and a prince who was in-between."

"Until he finds himself," Mrs. Prince nodded.

"Can't Priscilla help? I mean" ... apologetically ... "you did tell me that she and Bart —"

"I don't know, my dear. Really, I don't know much about any of my sons. Does any mother these days?" Mrs. Prince had finished with a laughing note before she repeated the business information she had given Verity upon her arrival.

"If you're agreeable you can start as promptly as tomorrow. Priscilla looks after the secretarial side. The buying, selling and display will be entirely yours."

"And Mr. Bartley Prince's?"

A little cloud as Mrs. Prince warned, "He never actually attaches himself here. I told you."

"Yet he is attached?"

"Yes, though not at the moment. He has been having a series of exploratory examinations in St. Martin's. When he does come back . . ." a rueful little laugh.

"He won't like me?"

"It's hard to say. My last effort when Bart was away was a bathroom setting, and all he said was 'Oh, Mother!' "

Now Verity laughed, too.

"One thing," Mrs. Prince went on, "I won't be here to hear 'Oh, Mother!' when he sees you. I'm leaving at once."

"Canada, wasn't it?"

"Yes, my sister's daughter is being married. I don't know how these mothers marry off their children. Don't forget, Miss Tyler, what I told you about that."

"I won't," smiled Verity.

She left soon afterwards, left for the little flat in Balmain that Robin had rather unhappily suggested.

"We can't have you here with us, you understand that, as Adele said we're married now."

"Of course, Robin. I understand perfectly. But I'd like to remain in Sydney a little longer. I won't get in your hair."

"You're a good scout, Verity. You always were," Robin had said awkwardly. "It's just that Adele thinks –"

"Adele is perfectly right. You must always think of her as right," Verity had urged with an ache in her heart. At the very least, she thought, let Robin not *know* Adele, the real Adele.

She had opened the attic window of the small apartment in the old terrace; Balmain was full of these charming nineteenth-century remnants of sandstock and iron lace. She had looked down on the shining green waterway of Johnston's Bay. Once, a century ago, the agent who had leased her the flat had told her, the bay had been full of American sail, for they had been allotted this portion of the harbour. In their ballast had come American earth and in some of the earth sprinklings of American seed. Houses had sprung up later on exotic flowers, stifling them, but there were still occasional strangers among the freesias and marigolds. Strangers. And that was what she was now, knew Verity, looking down on the bay, now that Robin was accounted for by Adele. She belonged to no one here, she was a stranger.

She smiled slightly at Mrs. Prince's fervent hope for a daughter-in-law and in time a grandchild. With Bart reserved for Priscilla, and from the difficult sound of him Verity did not envy Priscilla, there remained Matthew and Peter. A gracious prince. A charming prince. Which, she said flippantly to the green water, to choose?

She turned back to the small but adequate room and cooked

11

a small but adequate meal. After which she went to bed early as befitted the night before a new job.

But after she had switched off, and before she climbed into bed, she stood again at the attic window, looking down at lights now, hundreds of city lights reflected in the darkling water, for Balmain was wedded both to the harbour and to Sydney, golden ladders from soaring buildings, rainbow streamers from their neon lights.

For some absurd reason she was thinking of that old fairy-tale again. "Once upon a time there were three princes, a gracious prince, a charming prince, and a prince who was in-between."

Matthew, the gracious, she tagged. Peter, the charming. She finished rather drowsily: "Bart, the in-between," as she pulled up the rugs.

Though there had been no nine-to-five rule laid down . . . "In a place like Woman's Castle customers never come at nine but frequently linger after five," Mrs. Prince had smiled . . . Verity saw to it the next morning that she was on time.

The shop was one of a leisurely row of tasteful salons and boutiques, set in a small courtyard with its own miniature fountain. The street in which it stood was leafy and quiet and there were glimpses between the ornamental trees of Sydney Harbour. Apart from a tasteful sign in the form of artistically in-beckoning arms reading "Woman's Castle", there was no announcement and no display. Verity knew now that one had to enter for these.

The business was not actually opened, but the door was un-locked, so Verity went in. She could hear the tap of a type-writer, so crossed to the room from where the sound came. Here, too, the door was unlocked, on this occasion also ajar.

At her quiet knock, a girl got up at once, but in those few

12

moments Verity had time to look at Priscilla ... for it would be Priscilla ... and she liked what she saw. A serene girl. Could anyone ask for more? Brown-haired, brown-eyed, rather self-effacing, Verity judged. But if you received a first impression of plainness, the sweet smile that slowly took over the gentle face soon altered that impression. Verity found herself thinking with Mrs. Prince that Bart was certainly wasting time.

"Miss Tyler?" Priscilla asked pleasantly.

"Verity."

"And I'm Priscilla Burnett — Priscilla or Cilla or Prissie, I get them all. There was no need for you to get here this early, Verity."

"You're here," Verity pointed out.

"Accounts are different, they require office hours. Also I leave at five, and I'm afraid if you've a customer ..." Priscilla looked apologetically at Verity.

"Oh, I understand that perfectly. I worked in England in a business like this. But I must be honest: it wasn't as beautiful or expansive as this."

"It is, isn't it? That's Bart for you." Priscilla's eyes were soft and loving, and once again Verity thought — what holds that man up?

Already Priscilla was busy with teapot and packet of biscuits. "We have lots of short breaks here," she smiled, "Mrs. Prince loves time off for a natter, and Bart ... well, Bart just has to have time off." Again the gentle look.

"I'm looking forward to going through the shop," Verity proffered. "It's much larger than you might think from the front. I see there's an annexe at the back."

"Bart's collection of colonial and antique oil lamps. You'll love them. The trouble is they're not profitable."

"But surely people are interested —"

13

"Bart makes excuses not to let them go. Milk, Verity?"

Over the companionable cup, Verity learned more of the Princes. Matthew, the eldest, was just starting out in his first G.P. Woman's Castle did not see him very often, Priscilla confided, for you know how called-upon doctors always are . . .

Bart would account for himself when he came in, Priscilla said next, but when Verity suggested that that might also be some time away since he was in hospital, she corrected, no, it was a brief exploratory stay only, and he could arrive at any moment.

"That leaves Peter," said Verity. The charming prince, she thought to herself.

"Yes. Peter." Now there was something in Priscilla's voice that Verity could not pigeonhole for herself. She looked at the girl, but her expression remained as calm and gentle, there was simply nothing there to read.

"Will Peter come in?" she asked.

"You ask Peter and he won't be able to tell you," laughed Priscilla. But as she laughed with her, Verity wondered why she heard somewhere a bleak note in that laughter.

She learned that Priscilla was always busy on mail orders.

"Yet we don't advertise. It's just that once you buy from Woman's Castle it seems you always buy there. Customers move to the country, they go interstate, but they don't buy elsewhere. Then, of course, friends see their treasures and become customers, too. And so it builds up and up."

"Yet it has no one to keep it on – I mean not personally." Verity explained how Mrs. Prince had said several times that Bart, who was its present manager, had no real heart for the business, that he always considered himself as only on loan to it.

"That's so, but it still might have to be Bart's thing," said Priscilla in the loving voice again, "if that first indicative oper-

14

ation that Bart keeps on delaying comes out contra. I think that that is why Bart hesitates. While he doesn't know the truth, there's still hope. But he must submit eventually." She sighed. "Peter, of course, could do it. Peter can do anything."

"Except settle down? Oh, do forgive me. I don't usually gossip like this."

"It's not gossip, it's fact. You have to know more than the things you sell in a job to make it a success."

"Thank you, Priscilla," appreciated Verity. "Thank you, too, for the tea. Now I really must get to work. What time do I open the doors?"

"We don't. We leave them unfastened and customers just browse in as though it was their own house."

"That's perfect," applauded Verity. She took her cup to a sink in the corner of the office, washed, dried and replaced it, then went out to look around.

The shop was formed like the rooms of a house. She went from room to room, becoming progressively enthralled. There was a bathroom done in black and aqua. A kitchen in cherry red and white. A grey and coral lounge. An apple green dining setting. A bedroom entirely in white. Apart from these offices there was a purely antique room that she longed to explore, and beyond it the annexe she had spoken with Priscilla about, and where the secretary had said that Bart Prince housed his collection of oil lamps.

She went there first.

It was pure delight, she found – superb ruby, opaque amber and cranberry-coloured majolica, brass lamps, venetian lamps, iron, marble and copper. There were hanging lamps, bracket lamps, barn lanterns, conductor's and policeman's lamps, piano sconce lamps. – She had no doubt there were all the lamps of China.

In the antique room there were the expected treasures, yet

15

in this instance *very* treasured, Verity sensed. That French walnut bureau, for instance. That embroidery frame. The Georgian dropside table. The rouge marble wash stand.

She came out of the antique room to find there was a browser in the pretty kitchen setting. The women wanted a biscuit barrel. As a child she had always reached up for biscuits from a barrel, she related nostalgically, and now she wanted her children to do the same. Verity found a variety of barrels, one in floral china that the customer chose at once. – "Because," she said, "I change my colours around."

Closely following the biscuit barrel, she sold a jardiniere, and later in the morning a wall tapestry. The time raced and she loved every second of it, she told Priscilla at lunch.

After the secretary got back to her typing, Verity decided, business having drowsed away like the drowsy day, or so it appeared, to change a setting. At the Chelsea place at which she had worked they had changed the settings often, many customers laughingly complaining that barely had they time to get used to something than it was whisked away. However, the proprietor had believed in showing what he had, and every afternoon it had been Verity's job to re-set a room.

The sun porch in tawny golds seemed a likely change, and Verity decided to offer the customers a study in its place. A brown study, she thought, inspired.

She whisked away the gaily striped cushions and took down the sunflower curtains. The neutral furniture in the room, concealed before by gay covers and bright hangings, now lent itself to a more sober corner. Verity chose plain brown hopsack from a chest of drapes to hang at the mock windows, took the chintz off the table and left the table bare except for some books, a blotter sheet and a desk calendar, then she stepped back. Now was the time to add a touch of colour, she knew. One orange cushion, perhaps? Or a butter yellow? Or would

16

she keep to a bookish fawn?

She opened a cushion box and went despairingly through it, despairing because not one cushion seemed to fit the bill. She tried several, only to discard them at once, and was just sampling a muted green when a male voice behind her called: "No."

She turned round.

Her first impression of the objector was not one of height, and yet she saw that he was a tall person. She supposed it was the slight stoop that took away the inches – that, and a perceptible droop to the shoulders. The man was flint-hard, she also saw, but she received the impression that he had *forced* himself into this near-whipcord condition, almost a kind of challenge to what fate had delivered him. For the rest, she had only a quick impression of dark unsmiling eyes, dark unruly hair, and from the forehead to the beginning of a brown throat, a scar. It was, she thought at once, not a disfigurement, rather it was one of those flaws that seemed to make up a man's character.

"Seen enough?" The voice was cool, and Verity reddened. She searched for an apology that was not the usual trite excuse and during that moment he moved a few steps. He had a faint hesitation when he did so, not a limp so much as a deliberation, a pause.

Undoubtedly, Verity decided, it was Bartley Prince.

"I'm sorry." She gave up looking for the right apology.

He shrugged. "Excused. It does come as a shock at first."

"It does not," she came back. "I would have looked at anyone. You're my first customer this afternoon ... or so I thought."

That halted his deliberate movement. "*Your* first customer? Who are you?"

"The new assistant." She remembered what Mrs. Prince

17

had related about the bathroom setting, and added before she could stop herself: "Now you say 'Oh, Mother!' "

"Oh, Mother!" he obliged.

There was an awkward moment, then, meeting each other's eyes, they both laughed.

"I'm sorry you weren't told about me," apologized Verity.

"Now I know why my parent kept changing the subject when I asked about filling her void at Woman's Castle while she was away. Sly puss, that mother of mine. She flew out last night and knows I can't put her in her place."

"Woman's place?" As she said it, Verity glanced around her. Surely of all places Woman's Castle was a woman's place, she appreciated.

"Yet not this particular room," Bart Prince said drily, evidently reading Verity's thoughts. "A study is intrinsically a man's place. Are you naming it Brown Study, by the way?"

"Yes," she said, a little surprised.

"Then why are you cluttering it up with another colour?"

"Because – well, there should be a contrast."

"Should there?" He walked across and took the green cushion she still had in her hand and threw it away. "A brown study should be brown," he said. Then he ordered: "Look."

She looked and saw he was correct. She might have been taught about the necessity for a contrast but undoubtedly in this instance he was right. The room was right.

Across the distance between them, the green cushion still where it had been flung, she met his dark unsmiling eyes. Bartley Prince's eyes. Not the prince who was gracious, not the prince who was charming, but the prince who was in-between.

"I'm Bart," he said. "No doubt" ... the merest flicker of anger ... "you've gathered that already. And you?"

"Miss Tyler." As he still waited, "Verity Tyler," Verity said.

18

CHAPTER II

"AND do you practise it?" Bart Prince said lazily, almost un-interestedly as he bent down to pick up the cushion.

She knew what he meant, it often had been said to her, but nonetheless Verity replied, "If you mean truth —"

"I meant that."

"Then the answer is yes. Unless, of course, it would hurt someone."

"In which instance you don't adopt it?"

"No."

"Then little use my coming to you for truth then, is there? Unless" . . . a brief laugh . . . "not knowing me, you would be indifferent to hurting."

"I don't know you, but I couldn't be indifferent."

"In short a tender-hearted lady."

"Mr. Prince," said Verity carefully, "do you always look for rebuffs like this?"

"No, but I look for truth. Can you in truth look at me and not look away?"

"Yes."

"Is that being kind?" he taunted.

"It's being truthful. I think" . . . daringly . . . "you vastly exaggerate yourself."

To her relief, for she knew she had overstepped somewhat, he grinned. It was a fascinating grin. The slight scar gave it an amusing, rather lopsided, puckish look. He appeared much less intimidating.

"I suppose I do. We're all over-important to ourselves. My personal trouble is that it was trouble for nothing. If I could only lose that . . ." There was a brief return of the anger, then he shook it off. "Seen over the place?" he asked.

"It's beautiful. I worked in a beautiful business in Chelsea, but this is more so," she said sincerely.

"My father did it."

"Yet you carried it on." In her enthusiasm she forgot what Mrs. Prince had said.

He did not let her forget long.

"Only until such time as I can do a man's work," he said, and again there was that harsh edge to his voice.

Quickly she diverted, "I like your lamp section," and was rewarded by his eager smile.

"In the dictionary," he proffered a little diffidently, "it says simply that a lamp gives light. I know that it gave that to me – the collecting, I mean."

"And that's why it's unprofitable," she asked. "You won't part with it?"

"It gave me light," he said stubbornly, "when I was needing it. When I find another light, I'll be as mercenary as the rest. – Ah, Cilla." They had reached the office and he stopped to smile across at the secretary.

But not to smile across a room for long. At once Cilla came over and put her hand in his. "Bart," she said quietly.

He held the hand, put his other hand over it to seal the grasp.

"How was it in hospital?" she asked.

"Easier, knowing your gentle concern."

"Apart from that?"

"No results yet. They'll be given to Matthew."

"Oh, Bart!" As Priscilla looked lovingly at him, quite oblivious of Verity he leaned down and kissed her brow.

But he must have become conscious of Verity's rather embarrassed audience, for he tossed, "Pay no attention, it's a business practice."

To the sound of Priscilla's amused but reproving, "Oh, Bart!" again, Verity and the man moved on once more.

"You're not put off by the business practice?" he taunted as he led her into one of the displays.

"It didn't concern me," she said stiffly.

"But a business practice should concern all employees."

"One of such a nature presumably only concerns old employees."

"You mean ones who saw me Before, not just After?"

Verity stopped short. "Mr. Prince, I don't know how you were Before, but I can see how you are After, and I see nothing even remotely remarkable about it. But I do find something remarkable in the chip you carry. Even watching you carry it makes me tired."

Again she had overstepped herself, but she didn't care, she had to work with this man, so she must have an understanding.

There was silence for a while, then he said, "I asked for that. Peace, Miss Truth, pax, please."

"I don't like Miss Truth."

"I don't like Miss Tyler."

"Verity," she agreed.

"Bart," he smiled.

They went on.

"Why did you change my display?" he asked.

"In my former place of employment it was Rule One."

"Then it wasn't my taste that prompted it?"

"Your taste is quite perfect," she awarded coolly.

"Are you speaking professionally?"

"How otherwise would I speak?" she asked, surprised.

21

"I don't know. I haven't learned about you yet."

"You're a very odd man," she said indignantly.

"In that way as well as physically. I'm sorry" ... at once ... "no harping on the subject, you said."

"Yes, I said." To really close the subject, she crossed to a small, very beautiful Jacobean bureau. "Do you, like my former boss used to, advise young people to go without until they can get the best?" she asked professionally.

"You mean the best is worth waiting for?"

"Yes."

"But is it, though?"

She looked around her, at all the beautiful things. "Can *you* say that?"

"I often think it. You can wait for the best." He stopped a long moment. "And you can wait and wait." Without another word he turned and left the room.

"Odd," Verity awarded him again.

She heard him later in the office. He was laughing now with Priscilla, and she was surprised at the annoyance she felt at her own failure with him.

Shrugging, she went back to the front room to find a customer trying to make up her mind over a set of kitchen jars, so she helped her decide. After that she sold a small curved stool and a slender long-stemmed vase. Which all made it, she tallied, Priscilla having left now, a rather satisfactory day. As there were no more customers, she decided she could leave as well, but not knowing the ropes of the place yet she went in search of Bart Prince to ask his permission.

She found him where she had anticipated she would, among his lamps.

"Oh, yes, go," he nodded. "No need ever to ask."

"If there was a customer I would wait, but the street is empty."

"That's all right," he nodded again.

She hesitated, she could not have said why.

"How long do you stay, Mr. – I mean Bart?"

"Like the young people waiting for good furniture, I just wait," he told her.

"But seriously."

"I was serious."

"I really meant . . . well, could I fix you something?"

"Would you?"

The answer surprised her, but she said at once, "Of course."

"That's extraordinarily good of you, but no, thank you. I live in city digs with a handy restaurant. None of the Princes live at home. Matthew is now doing his G.P., Peter is here, there and everywhere, and I found it necessary to snare an apartment either on the ground floor or supplied with a lift. But" . . . with a meaning look at her . . . "we won't talk about that."

"But you are, aren't you? You keep bringing it back by apparently not talking about it. I'm sorry, I wish I could help."

"With fixing me up something?"

"No, with –" She stopped herself in time. "Good evening," she proffered, and went out.

It was a pleasant hour to leave, the office rush over, the rush to the city for the night's entertainments not yet begun. Verity went down to Circular Quay and caught the number five ferry.

The airy, green and white, "showboat" type of large launch that Sydneysiders still insisted on for their harbour transport was just drawing in. She boarded, then climbed the stairs to the upper deck. With a fuss and a flurry the ferry bustled off again, ignoring the more glamorous eastern aspect with its fine waterside houses to pass instead under the bridge and take the river way that the American sail once did. At the first little wharf Verity got off and climbed the steep hill.

When she got to her stone terrace house, she saw a car there, and eagerly she quickened her pace. It would be Robin.

Her half-brother was waiting in the flat for her ... she had given him a key ... and at once they ran to each other. For a moment Verity thought uneasily that it was not usually like this, it was not like Robin to show his affection in such a way – not, anyway, to her – and she searched his face, hoping her anxiety did not show.

He looked ill. She wondered if he had noticed it himself, but then ... and thank heaven ... it was the one to whom it happened who never noticed. One looked at oneself each day in the mirror and saw no change, or if you saw it, it was such a small change that it meant nothing at all.

But it meant a lot to Verity. She noticed bone structure in Robin's face she had never known before, a pull to his boyish mouth.

"How are you, darling?" She was glad she had always petted him and that now the endearment, almost fiercely felt, would not sound strange.

"Oh, fine, fine. I'm still a little below par after that 'flu thing, but then it was quite a bout, lots of people have been complaining that they haven't picked up. How are you, V?"

"Thriving."

"You look it." He gave her another hug. He had never been demonstrative, and it tore at Verity.

"Adele?" she asked as casually as she could.

"Beautiful. She is, isn't she? She's visiting an aunt tonight. That's why I'm here."

Verity restrained herself from saying, "Couldn't you have gone, too?" because she knew that Adele would not have been visiting an aunt at all. She made herself busy with cups and plates.

"Not for me, Verity," Robin declined.

"Eaten?"

"I'm just not hungry lately. This 'flu thing –"

"Yes, I know. It reacts like that. But some tea, surely."

"Tea," he agreed.

As she brewed it, he said abruptly: "It's not fair."

"What isn't, Robbie?"

"This place . . . I mean . . . well, it's so poor."

"Actually it's elegant. It's early colonial. If you don't believe me ask the agent who leased it to me," Verity laughed.

"Oh, it has a charm, I'll agree, but after our luxury apartment . . . I tell you, Verity, it's just not fair. Father was not fair. He shouldn't have left the entirety to me."

. . . Left what entirety? Verity secretly grieved.

"Oh, I don't know," she said casually, "you were his son."

"Yet you were the daughter of the woman he married to get that son."

"Robbie darling, he was a wonderful husband to Mother, he gave her everything. After she died, he gave me everything . . . the best of schools, of opportunities –"

"He didn't include you in the will, though, you didn't benefit."

. . . Who has benefited? Verity thought achingly for Robin.

"You were his son," she repeated stubbornly.

"Well, if you think like that, though I know I couldn't have thought so generously, keep it up, please, V. You see, Sis, now that I'm married, now that I have Adele –"

"Darling, I understand perfectly, a man must always put his wife first. Never think, or do, any other way."

"No," agreed Robin, "but sometimes the unfairness creeps in. I do worry, Verity."

"But why?"

"I with so much, you finding your own way in the world."

"You've changed, Robin." – He had. Once he never would

25

have thought of such things. Again Verity felt uneasy.

"Perhaps. I suppose it could be Adele. All I know is I worry where I didn't before. Or at least" ... a laugh ... "I think of someone other than myself." He looked fondly across at Verity.

"Then perish that thought, unless it's for your wife. I" ... in a sudden inspiration ... "have never been so – forward-looking in all my life."

"What do you mean, Verity?" When she did not answer, not knowing *what* to answer, wondering why she had made the rash statement, he said, "Is there someone, then? I mean is that why you're so – well, confident?"

"Could be," she evaded with a deliberate show of coyness.

"Like to tell?"

"I couldn't."

"I suppose not." A pause. "Could it be what Adele said recently?"

"What was that?"

"I was telling her where you were working. Prince's, isn't it? She said, 'Which one of the three Princes is she after?' Then she added, 'Any one of them would do.' I gathered," Robin smiled, "that money is no object there."

"No object," Verity said faintly.

"Then which?" he laughed.

"That would be telling," she came back. "Just leave it at that. Leave it at 'Once upon a time there were three princes.' Remember, Robin?"

"I remember. You were always one for stories," he recalled boyishly. "You used to read them to me, you were a wonderful reader, Verity. Yes, I remember 'The Three Princes.'" He smiled. "'Once upon a time there were three princes, a gracious prince, a charming prince –'"

Verity finished, "And a prince who was in-between."

26

"And which is it for you?" he persisted.

"Again, that would be telling." Better this, she thought, than to admit that there was no prince, nobody at all to keep her in Australia, except . . .

"Love – and the means, too," he commended, "what else can you ask? I'm always happy for Adele that as well as me she has expectations. I mean, it's a nice feeling for a girl, isn't it?"

"A nice feeling, darling," Verity assured him.

They drank tea together, but Robin ate nothing. She noticed the thinness of his fingers, the slight tremble as he held the cup.

When he left, he said, "You can't imagine how much easier I feel, Verity, I had no idea that you – I mean I thought you might just be staying on here for me."

She laughed at that . . . and hoped he did not hear a hollow note.

"But now that I know–" he went on.

"Robin, you don't know. I mean" . . . with concern, for after all a lie like this could have an unfortunate result . . . "I don't know myself."

"Verity, I'm not going to shout it out, I'm just going to re-peat to myself for my own peace of mind: 'There were three princes.'"

He was repeating it with amused satisfaction as he left her and went down to the car.

Well, it seemed a harmless fabrication, and if it appeased him, it satisfied her. She waved to the car as it left the kerb.

The next morning there was only Priscilla again in attendance at Woman's Castle, but Verity expected this would be the gen-eral rule, since as boss of the concern, for he was that even though he did not associate himself, Bart would need to be away frequently accruing more stock. She knew from the Chelsea shop how supplies must always be safeguarded a long way ahead.

She had a cup of tea with Priscilla, then got herself up to date with the goods in hand as she carefully dusted them. There were some beautiful pieces and the dusting was more pleasure than task.

Between the conning and the tidying, she sold a bed lamp and a tray, so felt she had earned her morning's salary.

After lunch she looked hard at the displays, not wanting to change them if they had been newly done. Priscilla, coming down the corridor, told her that the second bedroom setting had not been altered for some time, so she decided to change that.

But she voted against altering the purpose of the room, as she had altered the sun porch into a brown study. The study, she was pleased to see, was attracting much favourable attention. The only flaw was that it had not been entirely her inspiration. She would have added another colour and lost that brown impact.

She felt a challenge now to do something that was not added to or taken away from, and she stood regarding the minor bedroom a long time. It was a pretty setting in its present form, aimed at the gay teenager. Verity knew that she could not improve on it, so she decided to tackle a different age group.

She rummaged around the props, as it were, and inspiration came to her in the form of a very beautiful marcella quilt. From there on she unearthed more and more things that would be just right for the setting she had in mind – a Victorian bedroom for the older, more perceptive young woman, quiet, unassuming, in very good taste.

The plain narrow bed fortunately applied itself to the chaste scene. She removed every bit of bric-à-brac, but she allowed

28

small white linen mats under a brush and mirror set she also found in the big box. To her delight she unearthed an anti-quated washbasin and jug, remembering as she looked apprec-iatively at the flowered china that there was an appropriate stand in the back room storage. She had noticed it yesterday and admired the dark unpolished oak. She also recalled that it was on rollers, which would make it easy to wheel in.

Now she worked eagerly, with inspiration. She had always loved being urged on to an end she had in mind, but this time she found herself more anxious than she had ever been in Chel-sea. For it had to be right. Just right. She pressed in a final thumb tack to secure something, then sat back on her heels to regard the finished scene, for as far as she was concerned it was finished. Yesterday she had felt somehow uncertain, and the feeling had been right, for the room had not been right, but now she looked and was confident. But would he ... would Bart Prince ...

"Perfect," the man in the doorway said so certainly that there was no disbelieving the sincerity. Aware of ridiculous tears of relief, for they were ridiculous – this person's opinion could not matter that much – Verity scrambled to her feet.

"It's right?" she repeated.

"I said so." Bart Prince was looking at her quizzically, and, flushing, she looked away.

She hoped desperately that he would not query the anxiety she had so obviously betrayed. Whether he felt her sensitiveness or simply was not interested, he did not.

Together they left the setting.

"Tomorrow, Verity," Bart said, "the Castle will be closed."

"A holiday?" As a newchum she had not yet sorted out Australian festivals.

"The very opposite – we'll be working very hard."

"Stocktaking?"

"Stock gathering. I've had an offer from Lilith Vale, a small valley town on the other side of the Blue Mountains. I'm hoping to pick up quite a few treasures. Early colonials settled there on land grants."

"Can it be done in a day?"

"The distance there and back, yes, but not the examination of what offers. No, I'll take the van, and we'll stay overnight."

She opened her mouth to say something, then shut it. What she wanted to know was whom he meant by "we".

Deliberately, or so she thought, he misconstrued her unasked question.

"It has to be the van and a camp, there are no hotels at the Vale."

Now she moistened her lips. "There's no need to close shop. I can handle the business."

"Up at Lilith Vale?"

"You mean I –"

"I mean you come, too. Don't tell me" . . . impatiently . . . "you never left that Chelsea concern."

"Oh, no, I used to go buying with –" She had gone buying with Mr. Felix, but Mr. Felix had been plump, fatherly, and – well, Mr. Felix. They had also stayed in hotels. Mrs. Felix, too, had been with them.

He was looking at her quizzically again, but not sparing her this time as he had before.

"I do believe," he drawled, "you're that rare thing, a conventional female. I do believe, too, you don't want to come on that account." Before she could blurt something, though what it would have been she did not know, he said, "Be of good heart, Miss Grundy, Priscilla comes, too, of course."

"That's unfair," she said of his Miss Grundy, and to her surprise he agreed with her. She had noticed before that for all

30

his positiveness, suddenly and completely he could capitulate.

"It was just your uncertain little face," he grinned. "By rights a wreck like I am should take a bow, I suppose. But then" . . . hard and clipped again . . . "that subject is taboo. I must try to remember."

She did not comment . . . but she did wonder who had gone along with Priscilla on previous occasions. To her horror she heard herself asking: "Did you have an attendant here before me, Mr. Bart?" and heard at once his amused laugh.

"No. But Priscilla is entirely different. For that's what you're *really* asking, isn't it?"

She felt her cheeks burning. She could think of nothing to say.

"The van will call for you promptly at eight. Priscilla has your address. Please be ready." He turned and left her. Presently she heard him in the office, laughing with Priscilla. She wondered whether he was repeating her clumsy question and if they were both amused by it. It sounded as though they were exchanging something funny. Not feeling funny herself, feeling priggish and rather schoolgirlish, Verity was glad to see a customer enter the Castle, and she went forward at once.

The afternoon proved quite busy, for which she was very grateful, yet for all her absorption between her discussing and wrapping something kept coming back to her. It was Bart Prince's confident: "Priscilla is entirely different." She had known it, of course. Mrs. Prince had said it. The man's eyes as he had looked at Priscilla had said it. And now he himself had said it. Priscilla is entirely different. Suddenly and bleakly it came to Verity that at the age of twenty-seven, absorbed with Robin as she had always been, she had never been "entirely different" to a man. Any man.

Promptly at eight the next morning, as Bart Prince had said,

31

the van pulled up at the Balmain terrace. It looked a roomy vehicle, and when Priscilla moved up closer to Bart and Verity got in, she found there was ample space.

As it was the peak hour for morning traffic, little was said as Bart ably threaded his way in and out of cars. Verity decided that if it had been in a motor accident the man had sustained his injuries, then certainly his driving skill and nerve had not been impaired.

Because of Sydney's sprawl it was some time before they were free of the city. It must have rained through the night, for the paddocks on either side of the Western Highway were still wet. After they had passed Penrith and climbed up, there was a tantalising smell of woodsmoke from the mountain cottages mixed up with the tang of drying mountain earth.

Now the air was apple crisp, and it kept it up even after they descended from Mount Victoria, then proceeded along an offshoot ribbon of road. The minor track was narrow and bumpy but offering beauty at every turn, with the scallops of looming blue mountains between the leafy twigs of the bordering trees and the splashing streams.

A twist in the winding way and there was Lilith Vale: one old post-office hung with pink briar roses and no longer in use, one old courthouse, window-deep in encroaching sunflowers, and no longer in use, one old house, by the look of it barely in use, and that was it. "And after today, nothing in use," Bart said.

"What we don't take will be left to the possums," he told the girls. "Once Lilith Vale was on the main road to Lithgow, but many years ago, as you can see."

It had been a lovely old house, strictly in the early sprawling colonial style, plenty of space to stretch out, to breathe. Even now in its shabbiness there persisted that air of inbred pride.

Bart found a key in a prearranged place and they went in,

32

Priscilla at once busy on her notebook, the other two just gazing around them.

The rooms were rather low-ceilinged for their period, and the walls were panelled in dark rough wood. Because of the house's age the floor was buckled here and there and plaster had come down in several spots to lay on the planks like snow. The windows, as was usual in that era, were rather meagre, yet still extremely attractive, letting in sufficiently suffused primrose light to enhance the furniture that Bart had come about.

It was good furniture – simple, uncluttered and upon occasion quite lovely. There was a little cedar, a lot of mahogany and some warm old oak.

Bart called Priscilla and she made notes as he examined each piece.

Meanwhile Verity wandered round the house. There was no bric-à-brac; evidently only what could not be moved easily had been left. She wondered how Bart Prince would shift the stuff he decided to buy from the house, for like all old furniture it was heavy.

She browsed on . . . then all at once she stopped.

She had reached a fireplace, empty and cold, of course, but the width and depth and friendly accommodation of it somehow caught at her. She could see a family gathered here, a chair for the man of the house, a chair for the woman, a cradle for a child. She could see logs waiting that the man had cut, tea waiting that the woman had brewed. The child slept.

It was so real she could smell it, and hear it, and in her enchantment she half-turned as though to embrace it . . . and found herself breath-close to Bart Prince. He must have come in and in her absorption she had not heard him. What an idiot he must think her!

He did not speak for a long moment, then he put his hands out to the grate.

"Were you cold?" he asked, and she knew that he, too, was seeing the logs, the tea, the sleeping child.

Priscilla was calling out that a piece he had chosen appeared to have woodworm. Without another word, he went.

They had lunch from a hamper and a flask, then some men arrived in a utility to help Bart store the chosen pieces in the van. Verity was a little disturbed over this, for she had thought the inside of the van would be used as sleeping quarters, that the furniture would be consigned separately. Where then did they sleep?

She heard Bart arranging for the men to finish loading in the morning, and saw with surprise that this would be necessary, as already the sun was slipping away.

"Do we use the house tonight?" she asked Priscilla.

"No, it would be musty through being closed up – besides, Bart is a great one for stars." Priscilla gave that fond little laugh.

Bart drove the van to a small clearing he must have known about, and in an astonishingly short time had erected a tent for the girls and swung a hammock for himself.

"Now for tea," he said.

It was no hamper meal this time but steaks on green sticks, and damper. After they finished they just stopped where they were, talking idly, relapsing into comfortable silences, looking at the sky.

Then Priscilla, yawning widely, said that the mountain air always rocked her ... how often? Verity wondered, and with whom? ... and declared that she would go to bed.

Verity got up, too, but she did not cross as Priscilla did and lightly kiss Bart's brow, though Bart's bantering eyes challenged her to. It would amuse him, Verity thought, to be bid goodnight by *both* girls.

Inside the tent Bart had placed two inflated mattresses.

"They're wonderfully comfortable," Priscilla assured her, getting into sensible pyjamas.

Verity felt all varieties of a fool. Never having lived much of a social life, she had always expressed her instinctive femininity in pretty nightwear, fluffy concoctions like the scant apple green waltz-length gown she had brought now. She looked at Priscilla's cotton and then at her own gear with dismay.

"Oh, I'm sorry," regretted Priscilla genuinely, "I should have told you, Verity."

"I thought we'd be inside," Verity explained.

"I should have told you it would be canvas. Never mind, it's only tonight."

Priscilla was in bed by now, and grateful at least that Bart Prince could not see just how new was this newchum he now had in his employ, Verity stretched down on the pump-up and took up a magazine.

Priscilla had gone to sleep at once – she must have spoken genuinely when she said what the mountain air did to her – but Verity stayed awake for a long time.

At length she did feel a little drowsy, and decided to put out the lantern that Priscilla had left alight for her. Instead of getting right up, she leaned across, and in her inexperience she turned the wick up, not down, instantly flooding the tent with flaring light. Still uncertain which way to work it, not wanting to waken or alarm Priscilla, not at all happy over the ferocious leaping of the flame, she stepped carefully out of the tent with it . . . and into Bart Prince's arms.

"What in tarnation –" he began.

"I was frightened," she admitted.

"No need to be, the hurricane is foolproof, it won't start a fire." He took the lantern from her.

"I was frightened of waking Priscilla. She went to sleep at once."

35

"Presumably sleep is the idea." He was turning down the wick . . . and then he stopped. Without looking up at him to check, Verity still knew that now he was looking at *her*.

"You're a fool, Miss Tyler," he said at length.

"I'm sorry, I'm not used to lanterns."

"You're a fool to wear gear like that," he went on, ignoring the subject of the lamp. His eyes were taking in the soft revealing folds of the gown.

"You mean if fire did start . . ."

"Fire?" The way he said it she knew he had not been thinking that at all.

There was a long moment of complete silence. Not even the bush cracked. Not even a nightjar called.

"*Not* fire," he told her a little thickly, "man. A man can stand so much. Even my kind of a wreck of a man."

"Bart . . . Mr. Prince . . ." she stammered.

"Which I mustn't harp on. You've told me so."

Another silence, then:

"For heaven's sake, woman, get back to bed!"

CHAPTER III

In the week that followed, Verity often wondered if Bart Prince had really come to stand beside her at an empty grate to ask quietly: "Were you cold?"

Lilith Vale seemed a long way away now, much further than its seventy miles, as far away from Woman's Castle as the ends of the earth. The man was far away, too. She knew that a business background was totally different from a mountain one, but Bart Prince was more coolly remote than he had been when she had first started here, and, ruefully, he had not been exactly friendly then.

She wondered about it during her day's activities. Had he been so angry with her for not bringing a sensible sleeping suit, as Priscilla had, that he still rankled? But no, the following day after the lantern episode the subject had not been mentioned, and driving home had been pleasant enough.

But afterwards . . .

He was away a lot, and in his astringent mood Verity was glad of this. She had enough troubles. Robin had not been to see her, and though she disliked doing it in case she might be considered intrusive, she had gone to see him. Adele had been home.

It had been soon afterwards, she mused later, that Bart had come in and corrected very pointedly her new arrangement of wall panels. Before, his correction had piqued her, but she had seen how right he was, but on this occasion she had not seen it. He must have sensed her mortification, for he had reminded her blandly: "The boss is always right."

"I thought it was the customer."

"Which still makes me right, because this correction will ensure us a customer."

She had bitten her lip . . . and it had hurt . . . but much more hurting was the knowledgeable look he had given her, that knowledge that he was the boss and she could not answer back. Oh, why did she stay here?

Reading her in that uncanny way of his, he had agreed, "Yes, why? There are other jobs." Then, when she had not answered, "But you want *this* one, don't you?"

"I just want a job."

He had smiled thinly at that. It had been a disbelieving smile.

He had waited pointedly for a while, then he had inquired: "And for how long do you want 'just a job'?"

"I said I just want a job," she had answered flatly.

"For how long?" he had repeated. Mrs. Prince, his mother, had asked that, too, but very differently. "You came out to Australia to visit your brother, I hear," came next.

"I don't know how you heard that, but yes, I did. Only Robin is a half-brother."

"And a very comfortable one, I believe."

"Why should you believe it?"

"Isn't it true?"

It wasn't . . . but no one must know. "I meant how did you learn this?" she had corrected herself.

"The world," he had reminded her, "is a small place."

As she did not comment, he had said, "Among my acquaintance still on nodding and not wincing terms . . . sorry, I forgot, no self-pity . . . is Dellie."

As she looked at him in puzzlement, he said a little angrily, "Your half-brother's wife."

"Oh, Adele. Robin always calls her Adele."

"And you? What do you call her?"

"I haven't got to know her very well."

"So she remarked." His voice was dry, and he had said no more.

The next day they had classified his lantern collection, a fascinating business had he not been difficult again.

"A point, Miss Tyler." They had been pausing a few minutes; Verity had mused on the fact that he had been calling her Miss Tyler all the week.

"Yes, Mr. Prince?" she came back.

"I think it only fair to tell you that in a family of three apparently eligible males, there is actually only one eligible Prince."

She had gone a vivid pink. "And why are you telling me this?"

"Because of certain things –"

"What things?"

He had ignored that and continued, "Because of certain things I believe it would be wise. So often a girl wastes time, and if wastage can be avoided –"

"I don't care for your subject!" she said coldly.

"Nonetheless" . . . he had raised his voice . . . "*listen.* Matthew, though he won't admit it yet, is positively accounted for, even though the fool is not helping himself by adopting a wait-and-see attitude with Cassandra. Had I a raging beauty like Cassandra –"

"You would rush in where angels fear to tread? Is Matthew an angel? Your mother said he was a wonderful person."

"A wonderful idiot. But yes, Matthew is one of the best."

"Once upon a time there were three princes," said Verity absently, "a gracious prince, a charming prince, and a prince who was in-between."

"You go in for fairytales?"

"I did."

"It never dies out, I think — in which case, keeping a happy ending in view, forget Matthew, forget one of the other two, then keep strictly in mind that the field is reduced to only one."

Yes, Verity thought: Peter, the charmer. He is the sole one left if Matthew is written down for Cassandra, because you, Mr. Bart Prince, belong to Priscilla. She added to herself, rankling at his bald words: "Poor Priscilla!"

"I find all this in bad taste," she said aloud.

"It's in rotten taste, but it makes sense. If everybody was outspoken there'd be fewer broken hearts."

"I have no intention of breaking my heart," she told him.

"Or of breaking any other hearts?"

"You flatter me."

"I never flatter."

The next few days he was away. Verity, thinking it was business, never inquired from Priscilla, and was surprised one evening when the secretary asked her to visit Bart with her.

"Visit him?" she queried.

"He's in St. Martin's again. More tests."

"I didn't know." Verity had paused. "I hardly think he'd want to see me."

"Fresh faces," persuaded Priscilla. "Poor Bart gets terribly bored. Besides, even though he says he's not attached here, he's still very interested in how things are going. I can only tell him the clerical side. Will you come after we shut up, Verity?"

Verity, though not enthusiastically, agreed.

As the girls walked from Woman's Castle down the leafy street, Verity inquired from Priscilla as to what injury of Bart's was receiving the current attention.

"The leg. The doctors believe some of the drag can be eliminated — at least that's Matthew's report. Bart always persists that it's an examination to decide whether they'll take the leg altogether."

"Oh, no!" exclaimed Verity.

"No ... but that's how Bart gets. If only ..." But Priscilla left it at that.

If only he would let me share it all, Verity interpreted for herself. She asked if there was any other injury that was to be explored.

"No. Bart was in a very bad way, but everything else was patched up. Of course the scar will always be there."

"It's nothing," said Verity spontaneously. "I really mean if anything it lends something to him."

Priscilla turned quite radiantly to her. "I'm glad you said that. It's how I feel."

But not how Bart feels, thought Verity. "Can you in truth look at me and not look away?" he had said.

On an impulse, she took and pressed Priscilla's hand, and was surprised ... yet why should she be surprised? ... at the pressure the girl returned.

"I couldn't tell you what Bart means to me, has always meant," Priscilla proffered. "Without Bart ..."

"Then why don't you –" But Verity stopped herself at that.

They turned into the hospital, and Priscilla led the way unerringly down a maze of corridors ... "Yes, I come every day," she smiled, "so I should know" ... to a verandah room.

Because it was the leg that was receiving attention, Bart was propped up in bed. He looked very fit, though, and Verity recalled that his whipcord virility had been her first sharp impression of him, an impact of determined vigour in spite of what fate had dealt him.

Priscilla went at once to him and kissed his forehead lightly. He took her fingers in his. When he turned his glance to Verity, raising his brows as he did, he said, "The other member of

41

the staff! But not affording the same warm greeting."

"How do you do, Mr. Prince." Verity extended a cool hand.

"How do I do?" It seemed to amuse him. "I do well. The limb will remain with me a further week or so."

"Bart dear!" Priscilla's gentle voice reproached him, and he grinned and said, "Sorry, Cilla," and touched her fingers again.

"Sit down," he invited, his eyes now on Verity again, "and distribute the grapes."

"I'm afraid I didn't bring any," she said.

"No grapes?"

"I – well, as a matter of fact I didn't know you were in hospital until Priscilla told me. I mean" . . . for some reason becoming confused, and that fact annoying her . . . "you'd only just come out, and –" She knew that was the wrong thing to say, and he did not scruple to tell her.

"Didn't you know," he said harshly, "I have a permanent booking."

"Bart!" Again it was Priscilla.

"Sorry," he repeated. "I should remember, especially when I've been told how Miss Tyler doesn't like such conversation. What shall we talk about? Sealing wax?"

"There was a traveller called with a new furniture wax," related Priscilla equably. "Much less abrasive, I'd say. I thought on that last mahogany you bought –"

The talk veered to shop. When the hour was up, Priscilla again kissed Bart's brow . . . and Verity again extended her hand.

"I'll be back on deck again next week," he warned her, "so get your slacking over while you can."

"Bart, she never slacks," Priscilla objected.

"Only the boss."

"You most of all never do that."

"What's this now, then?" He looked down at the sheets. Then he glanced obliquely and ironically at Verity.

As they emerged from the hospital, Verity said, "Must he be so bitter?"

"It was very bitter for him."

"But lots of people are involved in bitter things."

Priscilla looked as though she was about to explain, then must have changed her mind. "It's Bart's story," she sighed, "not mine."

Yet your consequence, thought Verity, because of Bart's bitterness at what has happened to him, even though he loves you, the position is to remain at that. For now, anyway.

"Goodnight, Verity," Priscilla said, "thank you for coming, and that thanks is for Bart, too, for I don't believe he thanked you himself."

As she left the secretary, Verity thought that probably Priscilla had to perform a lot of social niceties for Bart Prince, but then Priscilla would not mind. What had she said? "I couldn't tell you what Bart means to me, has always meant." And then she had said: "Without Bart . . ."

A little bleakly, Verity boarded the ferry to Balmain.

She was pleased to see Robin's car drawn up at the terrace, but not so pleased, though she reproached herself over that, when, after opening up, it was Adele who greeted her.

"Hope you don't mind," smiled the girl . . . a smile for a change? . . . "but Robbie gave me the key. I suppose I could have sat in the car –" She shrugged.

"Of course you had to come in." Verity wondered unhappily if her voice sounded as false as she felt. No matter how hard she tried she could not warm to Adele . . . Dellie, as Bart had called her.

As she brewed coffee, she wondered why she didn't like her.

43

She was certainly a very attractive girl, but then only an attractive girl would have appealed to her half-brother. Indulged always, he had had the time and the means to look around.

But the means were almost gone now, she sighed to herself, and as for the time . . .

Almost as if she read her thoughts, Adele said: "He had another turn."

Her abrupt announcement, not even Robin's name spoken, choked at Verity, but she knew she could only harm Robin by being aggressive.

"What did the doctor say?" she asked, controlling herself with some great effort.

"The same, no doubt, as he said to you."

"Did Robbie question the attack?"

"No. He simply doesn't know because he never asks." The dark eyes, remarkably dark and large, rested on Verity. "That's what I've come about. He mustn't know."

This at least was one thing on which they could be agreed, and Verity said at once that she felt the same.

"For different reasons, though," suggested Adele thinly. "You're thinking of his peace of mind . . . well, perhaps I am, too, I'm not that hard, also I can't stand heroics – I mean, it would be awful to live with a man if he knew that."

The callousness of her shocked Verity, but in the shock she wondered how Adele would react if she told her more of the truth, told her of her husband's changed financial conditions. She could see the rising colour, the incredulous look, finally the mental checking of where she stood showing plainly in those lovely eyes, and then the girl turning and walking out. Walking out from Robin as well. No, Adele must not know. If Robbie lasted longer than the money lasted, she must still not know. Somewhere I'll get money, Verity thought. I don't know how, but Robin . . . my Robin . . .

"I also don't wish Robin to know because lately he has become quite concerned over you," Adele said coldly. "I have no doubt," she went on, "that faced with that he could get quite maudlin, even wish to make a future settlement on you."

"That's absurd!" Absurd in more ways than you think, Verity could have added. Aloud, she reasoned, "It was his father's money. I wasn't his father's child."

"No, and evidently it hasn't worried him until now. There is an obvious solution, you know. Why don't you go back to England?"

"We had that out before," said Verity dully. "I can't go until – until Robbie goes. I've always loved Robin."

"Yes." Adele yawned. "He's told me countless times how you practically reared him. Quite touching ... so long as there's no other motive."

"You're an unrewarding person, Adele," Verity said with considerable restraint.

"I haven't enjoyed the most rewarding of experiences." The girl lit a cigarette, and Verity saw the line to her mouth and thought yes, that would be so, and she's let it harden her.

"Anyhow, we two are agreed," she shrugged. "If not about your return to England, perhaps, then about not letting Robin know. Of course" ... another shrug ... "we wouldn't actually see you stuck, at least I won't see you stuck. But you're doing quite well, aren't you? Anyone would – with the Princes."

"I believe you know them."

"Most Sydney people would, if only by repute. They're very rich. Riches seem to broadcast themselves." Adele laughed. "Which one are you setting your cap at? Financially they would all bring the same reward."

"Do you have to talk like this?" jerked Verity.

"You don't like truths?"

"It's not the truth."

45

"Time will tell," smiled Adele. She glanced at her watch. "Is that the time now? I must go."

She went without any more discussion, and as soon as the car moved away from the kerb, Verity came back into the house, left the door open, pushed wide the windows, let the wind come in. She felt stifled.

She did not visit Bart any more, and one morning, asking Priscilla a little offhandedly how he was, learned from the secretary that she was not visiting him either, since he had left St. Martin's and was undergoing some remedial treatment at an out-of-town clinic.

"That's the pattern for Bart," Priscilla said regretfully. "Perhaps one day he won't need these attendances. Matthew believes so, anyway."

"How long will he be away?" Verity asked.

"As long as they can prevail upon him to stop — but he can be very stubborn."

Yes, thought Verity, you of all people would know that.

"Matthew is a clever doctor, his mother said," she said instead.

"He graduated very highly. But like all the Princes, he's extremely obstinate. He has the means to set up a successful practice — all the sons have their own means."

Yes, thought Verity, remembering Adele, financially they would all bring the same reward.

"But Matthew wouldn't be content with that," Priscilla went on. "He must earn his own way, he thinks. He has taken this practice in an outer suburb, a suburb with a distinctly industrial slant, so you can guess how busy he'll be. While he works his way up he won't avail himself of any of his inheritance. He feels the manner he's doing his thing is putting him on his mettle."

46

"And does Cassandra ... oh, yes, I know about Cassandra ... think that, too?" They were having coffee, and coffee was a time for confidences. But perhaps this one was too close for comfort, for Verity noticed that Priscilla went a dull red, that she looked uneasy.

The girl did not speak for quite a while, then she asked Verity: "And what do you know about Cassandra?"

"Only that she's beautiful."

"Yes. Beautiful." Again the strained look.

Now Verity believed she knew what was worrying the secretary. Bart had spoken enthusiastically about Cassandra's loveliness, and seeing that he had said it to her, Verity, he must have also said it at some time to Priscilla. She looked sympathetically at the girl.

"Yes," sighed Priscilla again, "beautiful. She's all that Bart described."

"Bart also said," repeated Verity, hoping to cheer Priscilla, "that Matthew was a fool not to rush in."

"It wasn't Matthew I was thinking of," Priscilla said wretchedly. She pushed her cup aside and walked the length of the room.

"Have you ever guessed," she broke in abruptly, "the misery of being a plain girl?"

"All my life," answered Verity candidly.

"You?" There was no denying the surprise in Priscilla's voice. "Don't you ever look in a mirror?" At Verity's blank face, she went on, "No, perhaps you don't know that you're attractive – some girls are like that, and it is, I think, their main attraction. But look, please, at me, plain Priscilla, without any attraction."

"The eye of the beholder," refused Verity definitely. "You have a sweet serenity that wins through, and I'm sincere about that."

"Well, little good it's done me," sighed Priscilla.

"But your position is quite different, isn't it, your – well, your man is different."

"Yes," said Priscilla quietly, "my man is very different."

"Then why are you worrying? Why is Cassandra concerning you?"

"Because she's everything you heard. I . . . I'm not a jealous person, Verity. For instance, I can't be jealous of you. But Cassandra . . . well, I just don't know," she sighed.

Verity wished she could find the right words for her, but what were the right words? She waited a while, then went back to work.

It seemed odd after their talk that the subject of the talk should make herself known that afternoon. Cassandra called in.

Though she had been told the girl was lovely, Verity still experienced that sudden sharp impact that beauty does to you. For Cassandra was *very* lovely. She stood at the door smiling at Verity, and Verity knew at once that she must be Cassandra, knew it because beauty, beauty such as Bart Prince had described, was a rare thing, and this girl had it.

Cassandra's colouring was magnificent – bright copper hair, the white skin that sometimes goes with it, a naturally scarlet mouth. Verity looked at her in admiration, thinking how mousy her own acorn top and acorn eyes must seem in comparison.

However, there was a debit side to the beauty. Cassandra had none of Priscilla's quietude and composure, that trait that Verity had told the secretary in her opinion won through. Also, there was a certain discontent in the lovely eyes, a frustration, a restlessness. She seemed vaguely unhappy, and perhaps because of that unhappiness there was a slight challenge, a touch of recklessness there.

But the smile now was genuine; there was an obvious anxiety to be friendly. This girl, for all her beauty, is lonely, Verity thought. She smiled back.

"Cassandra, I think."

"Now why would you think that?"

"I was told you were a beautiful girl."

"Oh, please!" There was no coyness in Cassandra's appeal, she meant it. Verity could see that often her beauty set her back.

"I'm the new girl," Verity introduced herself, "name of Verity Tyler."

"I'm glad to meet you, Verity. Thank you for greeting me. Priscilla" . . . a little troublously . . . "does, but doesn't, if you understand."

Verity fully understood, but she doubted if Cassandra did, Cassandra would never remotely understand how Priscilla would feel about her man, or her man she one day hoped, saying, "She's beautiful."

She cleared a chair and invited Cassandra to sit down. For a few minutes they talked shop, though not very astutely. Cassandra, Verity could see, was pleased but by no means enchanted with rare things. Why should she be? she thought wryly. She was a rare thing herself.

"All very lovely," agreed the lovely girl, "but I must admit I'm a realist. I'm like that American I read about, who remarked of the vanishing wildlife in the American Everglades that he didn't think about alligators, he thought about people." She looked moodily out of the shop door at snippets of harbour dancing between the leaves of the trees. "I like people," she said. As Verity waited, she went on, "I'm a nurse, but not a brilliant one, I'm afraid. I didn't join out of dedication but because . . . again . . . I like people."

"Surely reason enough. Are you still nursing?"

"I graduated," said Cassandra but without pride, "and I

take on relief jobs. You see I did hope to . . ." Her voice trailed off.

Now another one, thought Verity, another girl emotionally tied to a Prince and Prince doing nothing about it. Bart and Priscilla. Matthew and Cassandra. In Bart's case, it was his health. In Matthew's case, it was his career. How much of a fool can a man be?

"I met Matthew nursing," said Cassandra. "Have you met Matthew?"

"I've only met Bart," Verity told her.

"Bart is sweet." Cassandra took out and lit a cigarette.

"Yet as stubborn as Matthew," Verity dared.

"Bart? No, I wouldn't think so."

He must be, decided Verity for herself, otherwise he would not be holding out from Priscilla as Matthew is holding out from you.

"It's Matthew who's the stubborn one," Cassandra told Verity. "He must be established before he . . . well, before . . ." She got up restlessly to pace the room, take things up, put them down again.

"I'm going away," she said abruptly. "I have had the offer of a temporary post in Melbourne. I have accepted it. I think it might do good."

Do good for you or Matthew? wondered Verity, but aloud she murmured that a change was always advisable.

"Well, we'll see." Cassandra did not sound very hopeful. She looked at Priscilla, now standing at the door and offering coffee. She smiled at her, and Verity could see the distinct effort it cost Priscilla to smile back. Bart was a fool, she thought angrily, to worry this sweet girl like he did. Why didn't he . . . Then why didn't Matthew . . .

It seemed that only Peter Prince stood outside the tangle.

"You can tell Bart I've gone," Cassandra said in the office.

50

"You can tell – Matthew if you see him."

"How long will you be away, Cassandra?" It was Priscilla.

"I don't know." Cassandra's voice seemed tired.

She went soon after that, and the rooms filled with beauty were less beautiful without her.

"Well?" asked Priscilla.

"Yes," agreed Verity, "she's the loveliest girl I've ever seen."

She was busy for the rest of the day. No time for display altering, even for dusting. Customers came and bought. She was there long after Priscilla had gone, having assured the secretary that she should leave, that there was nothing here for her to do, that this was what an attendant expected, and, when sales were being won, really enjoyed.

Verity had wrapped up an etching, her final transaction, and accompanied the buyer to the door with the intention of closing up at last, when one more customer, or customer she thought, came in. Well, it didn't matter, there was only the empty flat to go home to. She turned to the man . . . and gave a half step forward. Bart.

Then she saw it wasn't Bart, though a strong family resemblance was still there. Yet with a difference. This man was infinitely more sophisticated, more carefully tailored; there was none of Bart's whipcord strength, that strength that always seemed so carefully, so jealously guarded, as though it was all he had left. Peter. She supposed it must be Peter, for he was obviously younger, not older, than Bart. He was also better looking. There was no slight scar. As he moved forward, she noted no hesitancy. He was what Bart might have been and wasn't. – He was the charming prince.

Peter Prince for his part saw a girl in a pastel overall, pale brown hair, pastel colouring to match. A cool pretty girl.

"Cassandra," he claimed. "They told me you were a beauty, but they didn't tell me enough."

51

"They?" she queried.

"Matthew. Old Bart."

She did not say she did not believe that of Bart, she simply corrected: "Then they told you about someone else. I'm not Cassandra."

"Then –?"

"Verity Tyler," she introduced, "I work here."

"Verity." At once he discarded the Tyler. "Meet Peter, the third Prince." He bowed.

Once upon a time there were three princes ... Verity was thinking this as she put her hand into his. He enfolded it with his other hand, kept her hand there. She did not try to withdraw it. She stood smiling back at him. The fairytale was true, she thought a little headily, trying not to be carried away, but – being carried.

He was the most charming man she had ever met.

CHAPTER IV

NEVER had Verity been so late leaving Woman's Castle. She had sat talking with Peter Prince until the lengthening shadows had told her it was time ... and more than time ... to lock the doors. When she had done so, she had come back to Peter now in Priscilla's office, and brewing coffee with the air of someone who knew his way about.

"Oh, yes," he said breezily, "I always help myself here, Verity." His bright blue eyes flicked across at hers.

She found biscuits, and they sat and talked again. Talked and talked. He was the easiest man to talk to she had ever met.

When he said in a pause of the conversation that it was after eight, she looked at him in amazement.

When he said also, "You're having dinner with me," she did not protest.

Verity went into the washroom and took off her overall, wishing she had something smarter to wear than her utilitarian navy suit. She had a scarf, though, and tucked it at her throat. She loosened her straight acorn hair, let it hang free. She put on more lipstick than she usually wore. When she came out he was waiting for her, and he looked her up and down. He said in a voice that caught sharply and deliciously at her: "You're an English rose."

She flushed at the compliment, and in Priscilla's mirror saw that she *was* looking pretty – never a Cassandra, but appealing and nice to be with. He seemed to find her nice to be with, anyhow. He extended his hand and she went to him.

"Goodnight, old Prissie," he said to the office ... and it was the first discordant note.

"Why do you say that?" Verity asked, not caring for the feeling his carefree words had given her.

"Oh, I know Pris isn't old, no older, my rose, than you, but she is a solemn stick, isn't she, and bless her for it. We must have a sobering touch. Now, where shall we go?"

He chose an Italian restaurant, a very intimate place with red-checked tablecloths on secluded tables for two. He ordered heady wine, ravioli and a delicious salad. He also ordered a string of personal songs for the wandering musician. Verity, seeing the banknote he took from his pocket, protested, but he silenced her with a finger on his lips.

"Quiet, rose."

She was quiet.

It was a delightful evening. After he had left her at the flat, not spoiling anything by hurrying the magic moment, being content merely to touch her cheek with light lips. Verity knew she had never had such a night.

She stood at the window a long while, looking out on the glittering bay, for the first time in a long time not thinking of Robin, of Adele, of Woman's Castle and those who attended it, not even remembering the impact of the beautiful Cassandra ... Bart ... just thinking of Peter, the youngest Prince, the charming prince.

Well, she smiled, not far from enchantment, if nothing more ever happens to me, that's enough for dreams.

The next day she knew she had only just begun.

Peter was at Woman's Castle before she was. The first she saw of him was his swinging leg, swinging as he perched on Priscilla's desk and no doubt teased the secretary abominably. What had he said? "She's a solemn stick, and bless her for it." Verity wondered how Priscilla felt about that.

But when she entered, and Peter jumped off the desk and came across to greet her, bowing low in exaggerated chivalry as he kissed her hand but his upturned eyes telling her unmistakably that he was kissing her mouth, there was no question how Priscilla felt: she was not happy over the little scene.

Not understanding the secretary's cool attitude, for after all Peter was a free agent, Verity said weakly, "I didn't expect you here, Peter, or at least so early. Good morning, Priscilla. No need for you to introduce the third Prince. I met him last night."

"I see," said Priscilla drily.

Oddly uncomfortable, and why should she be, Verity hung up her coat and put on her smock. She was grateful that a customer entered, and, excusing herself, she went into the shop.

But Peter followed her. He not only followed her, he helped her with the sale. Verity was sure the customer bought more than she had intended. He was indeed the charming prince, she thought.

It was a busy morning. She had no time to talk to Peter. In the end their only interchange was over the midday snack, when Peter, still around, accepted one of the sandwiches that Priscilla had made, and said to Verity: "Tonight again? We'll try an Indonesian offering."

A little embarrassed, yet telling herself once more she had no need to be, that she was speaking to Bart's girl, even though Bart, according to his mother, and according to what she had seen, was doing very little about it, Verity said, "Perhaps Priscilla would like to come."

Priscilla's "No, thank you" and Peter's laugh came at the same time.

"I have an engagement," Priscilla said.

"Old sobersides," said Peter.

All the afternoon Peter stayed with Verity. They were busy, fortunately. Otherwise, Verity knew, Peter would have been doing more than help clinch a sale. There was no doubt about it that he had a talent for clinching sales. His mother had said that. Mrs. Prince had said that Peter, whatever he chose, would skate through.

Now he was skating through the afternoon hours, selling more with his easy charm than Verity knew she would with her knowledge and training. At half past five he called, "Down tools, Verity Tyler!"

"I never go till after six," she told him.

"Tonight you go now. I hope you're not tired, for we're dancing as well as dining, my girl."

"At an Indonesian restaurant?"

"Ever heard of the Tanka Bushi?" he laughed.

There was no one at the door. Verity peeped out and saw that there was no one in the street. A little self-conscious ... though heavens, why should she be? ... she went into the office and told Priscilla, who had evidently decided to work late, that she was leaving.

"Yes," was all Priscilla said.

Just as last night, the night was pure enchantment. In Peter's arms, as they tried the national dance, Verity felt a throb she had never felt before. But then she had never met a man like this man before.

"And I thought you were Cassandra," he said once.

"Cassandra is beautiful."

"You're a rose. You know" ... a confiding smile ... "I was always one for the glamour blooms – orchids, liliums, the rest. I never thought I'd lose my heart to a hedgerose."

"Oh, Peter!" she protested.

"It's true, darling." – Darling?

"You hardly know me."

"It's long enough," he assured her.

"Things don't happen so quickly ... I mean not lasting things."

"This will."

Yes, she thought in her heart, *this* will. It must be going to last, her heart ran on, because everything else is pushed out of my mind. I think of no one but Peter. Even Robbie has receded. Adele. Priscilla – Bart. Bart, the prince who was in-between.

"Darling, what are you thinking?" Peter asked.

"Actually of your brother."

"Matthew or Bart?"

"I haven't met Matthew."

"Then you were thinking of Bart." Peter made an absurd gesture of nervousness.

"Why do you do that?"

"Can't say really. All I know is he's the only one who ever scared daylights out of me. Did as a kid. I was a forthright youngster. I stood my ground – stood it with my mother, Matthew, all my teachers. But never with Bart. Even after the accident and Bart less ... well, less than what he had been ... that boyo still had the upper hand. I admire him to the ends of the earth, but let's not talk about him. He's safely out at the clinic, isn't he?"

"Yes, Peter," said Verity, a little puzzled.

The next night they tried a new restaurant. The music was soft, intimate. And soft and intimate was Peter's hand on Verity's hair.

"It's thistle silk," he said.

She did not pull away, she wanted his hand to stop there for ever. She wanted Peter to stop beside her for ever. She wanted to trap this moment and keep it for ever. She felt as frail as gossamer, as insubstantial as the thistle silk he had called her hair. Time counted for nothing. The world around her didn't matter, nor Robin, nor Adele, no one in the world, save Peter.

She was aware of an elation she had never known before. It was enchantment, it was magic, it was unreality ... but after it she wanted no reality.

Across the table her acorn eyes met Peter's blue ones. For all the strong family resemblance Bart had brown eyes, not blue ... but why had Bart occurred?

"It is true, isn't it?" Peter was smiling.

"What is?"

"That you feel like I do."

Verity tried to say, "And what is that?" but found she couldn't.

Instead she listened to Peter, Peter the charming prince, Peter saying: "So short a time ... almost only hours ... but darling, Verity my darling, already I believe we care."

I know *I* care, Verity said that night to the glittering bay, for she knew she had never felt like this before in her life. There had been men friends between her gentle guarding of Robin, and for some she had felt more than companionship, but never had she felt the excitement, the sweet madness that she did with Peter. If a feeling of gay rapture meant caring, then she knew she cared very much.

She gazed long out on Johnston's Bay, and the silky stillness was almost tender.

Then a little tug busies itself across the water, only visible by its winking light. It was quite an unimportant tug, but it left behind it a widening circle of shining ripples. And into Verity's new uncaring happiness, like a pebble flung into a pond, came the widening circles of an odd disquiet, a *Bart* disquiet: unmistakably she knew it, for how could Bartley Prince keep out of this? How, she thought uneasily, would he react?

She stood on, telling herself it had nothing to do with Bart Prince, that love had nothing to do with anybody save the ones it concerned, but it was no use. There was something about Bart Prince . . .

She forgot all about it the next day, though, with Peter in attendance once more and Priscilla becoming more and more withdrawn.

They had dinner at an Indian restaurant this time, laughingly competing as to who could eat the hottest spices, then sobering suddenly and sweetly as their eyes met and held . . .

It continued, Priscilla still standing remote, all the week.

Then –

Unannounced, unadvised, just as he had before, Bart came back. Verity was hand-rubbing a piece of rosewood and she knew who owned that slightly, very slightly shuffling step without looking up. But she did look up. It was Bart.

Guiltily, and hating herself for it, for what had she to be guilty about, she said, "How are you, Mr. Prince?"

"That can wait," he said abruptly. "Where's my brother?"

"Peter?"

"You know it isn't Matthew."

"He – he's not here."

"When do you expect him?"

"I expect him?" she echoed.

"You heard aright. When?"

". . . Well, he's been coming in around eleven."

"Why didn't you say so at once?" Before she could answer, he went off.

Almost immediately Peter arrived, and with a wave, since a browser had entered with him, he crossed to the office before

59

Verity could warn him. At once voices were raised inside the office, and Verity discreetly closed the intervening door – but not before she heard the first fragments of a heated discussion. Mainly Bart's fragments, for Peter evidently found it hard to state his case.

. . . "Since when have you become so interested in Woman's Castle, Peter?"

. . . "If you really mean you want to try out this business you'll have to serve your cadetship like anyone else."

. . . "You'll go interstate, as I did, like it or not – good lord, man, who do you think you are?"

. . . "There's no short cut, no easy way, and if I accept you, *if*, you'll do what I tell you, work where I say."

"No, Peter, there's no alternative."

Yes, mainly Bart.

Then, breaking in at last, Peter's answers, undoubtedly protesting that he did not want to leave Sydney, that he wanted to work right here.

Bart still saying he must go.

And suddenly, surely, the fact coming to Verity that Peter *would* go, because Bart, for all his weakness, was strong. Stronger than Peter ever would be.

Later she heard Peter leave, no goodbye, just a quick appearance at her door . . . she was serving the browser now . . . and his finger on his lips to her in farewell.

"Did Peter . . . did Mr. Prince . . " she started to ask Priscilla later.

"Yes, Bart sent Peter interstate," finished Priscilla for her. "That is, if Peter is serious, and if he wants a future like this." Priscilla glanced indicatively around. "If he doesn't, then he can please himself, but otherwise he'll do what Bart says. Bart always wins, you know."

"I didn't know. I know now."

"Yes, you know now." It was Bart Prince at the door. "That last sale, Miss Tyler," he told her formally, "you very nearly lost. You can stay back after we close tonight and I'll suggest to you what you lack."

It sounded a suggestion, but Verity knew it was an order, an order she dared not disobey.

Priscilla had made no other comment. She had lost her withdrawn air and now she looked almost sorry for Verity. Well, Verity thought, not very happy for herself, even someone who loved Bart as Priscilla did would never take him lightly.

She spent more time over her last customer than the customer's two Japanese candles deserved. But at last she could eke out the moment no longer, and she was listening to Bart follow the customer to the doors to drive home the bolts.

He did the closing up slowly, deliberately, double checking. No thief, Verity thought abstractedly, would find it easy to break in here tonight.

Then he turned, slowly, deliberately again, to look at Verity.

"Well, Miss Tyler?" he said.

She pretended puzzlement, though she knew it would be no use, there would be no subterfuge with this man.

"I want an explanation," he said barely.

"I made the sale," she defended. "Sometimes it's like that, some customers aren't so easy as others, some – Mr. Prince!" For Bart had come across and taken her hand, and his grip was punitive.

He still did not release her, even though he must have seen her wince. "Stop misunderstanding me," he said. "You know what this is about."

She wanted still to pretend confusion. What right had this man to intrude like this? She wasn't hurting anyone, but one look at his angry face changed her mind.

61

"Yes, I know," she admitted instead.

"Then get any fancy ideas you may have right out of your head. You're not for my brother Peter."

"You could have put it that your brother Peter was not for me." She had gone a dull red.

"Put it whatever way you like, so long as you get the idea."

"I don't get the idea, as you put it, and I resent you speaking like this!" she snapped.

"You'll resent it a great deal more if you go any further."

This was too much! What did he think he was, his brother's keeper? Who was he to forbid love? She was not aware that she had said it aloud until he answered roughly, "Love! Don't give me that. You don't love Peter, and Peter —"

"Yes? Peter?"

"Peter is already accounted for," he said bluntly.

"Then that's something he doesn't know." But she was aware of a tension in her, a tension and *not* a confidence. It should be a confidence, she knew that, a confidence in what Peter had whispered to her. But now, when she wanted it, she could not gather any confidence to her. It simply wasn't there.

He was looking at her shrewdly, summing up her doubt. She wished she could wipe that small smile off his face, tell him he was wrong. — Yet was he wrong? Was Bart? And what about herself? How much had Peter meant ... that is, apart from that new enchantment, that new sweet madness? How much had he meant?

Peter is already accounted for.

For the first time she seemed *really* to hear Bart's words. Before, Bart had said that there was only one available Prince, and she had taken it to be Peter. If what Bart said now was true, then the only one must be — Bart. Matthew had already been discussed and dismissed. But Bart — why, Bart belonged ... His mother had said so ... Priscilla's soft eyes had acclaimed it ... Yet Bart, in Bart's own words, was the only Prince to remain.

"So the episode is now finished," Bart Prince was saying authoritatively. "It would have been, anyway, because I've sent Peter off."

"Yes, I heard you."

"And with my brother Peter it's out of sight out of mind. I'm really doing you a service, preparing you for a letdown in this way."

"Then thank you, Mr. Prince, for the service." She was looking round for her coat. She hoped he did not see that she was trembling.

But the keen eyes missed nothing. Abruptly, quite unexpectedly, he said: "Will you have dinner with me?"

"No."

"Yet you went ... frequently ... with my brother."

"That was different. You're my employer."

"Possibly Peter could be in the future. We'll discuss it over the meal."

"I still don't wish to come."

"If I make it an order?"

"When you make an order you don't make a question of it."

"Put on your coat," he said, and he went across, got the coat and handed it to her. For a moment she hesitated, saw there was no question in him now, and slowly, unwillingly complied. He barely touched her elbow and together they emerged into the street.

Peter's restaurants had been carefully chosen, Peter had studied the menu, conferred with the chef. But Bart simply led Verity to the end of the street to a small simple room with a red door beneath a red awning. At a window table he shrugged carelessly over the offerings, leaving it eventually to the waiter. When the waiter had gone, he pushed aside the plate in front of him and put his elbows there instead.

"You've been a fool," he began.

"So it's to be that sort of dinner!"

"You didn't think I brought you here to feed you, did you?"

"You could have done your talking back at the Castle."

"Propriety," he reminded her coolly. "Behind closed doors. Though that hasn't worried you, has it?"

The first dish arrived, and in spite of everything it was delicious. It was a good restaurant. She said so, surprised, and he said, equally surprised, "Where else did you think I would have taken you?" After what he had just said about the type of dinner she was to receive, all Verity could think was: What a man!

They did not speak much until the waiter had removed the final plates, then Bart Prince said: "I want your promise."

"Yes?"

"To drop this fool affair now."

"You mean Peter?"

"I don't mean Woman's Castle."

"What business is it of yours?" she demanded.

"All my business."

"Your mother —" she began.

"My mother has three sons she loves but doesn't understand."

"She told me that she —"

"That she wanted you to nab one of the Princes, or something to that effect — oh, yes, that would be my mother. But the thing she did *not* say was to rule out the first and last."

"That leaves the in-between." Now Verity spoke out what she had thought . . . and incredulously . . . before.

"Precisely. Any objection?" His eyes were narrowed on her.

When she replied, it was not an answer for herself, but for Priscilla.

"There could well be, Mr. Prince."

"Namely?"

She stared at him in dislike. How could he use Priscilla as he did?

When she did not answer, for indeed she was so disgusted she was incapable of answering, he said sneeringly, "Why these evasions and innuendoes? Why that 'There could well be, Mr. Prince'? Why not come straight out and say, 'Yes, I would object.' Why, Miss Tyler?"

"Can we drop the subject?" she asked distastefully.

"And take up the subject of Peter?"

"Why not? Peter and I –"

"Have nothing," he said baldly.

"You could be wrong."

"Only I'm not."

"How could you know – I mean –"

Bart did not lean across the table, but all the same his eyes seemed to move forward to meet hers. "I know," he said quietly, and while hating him for that, she knew suddenly and with bitter chagrin that he did know. Why . . . oh, why had she had this change of heart? Or had it been only change of mind?

Angrily she cried, but secretly in challenge not conviction: "I care about Peter."

Bart smiled thinly and said nothing.

Needled now, she flung: "He cares about me."

This time he laughed scornfully. "*That* I do know about."

"And what is it you know?"

"That Peter has already near-forgotten you. I'm sorry, I mean I'm sorry if you're hurt, but that's our Peter."

"You're not a loyal brother," she said sarcastically.

"I am an aware brother, aware of Peter's –"

"Failings? And they would include me?"

"Your words, Miss Tyler, but since you put it that way,

65

yes. Peter is – what shall we say? – vulnerable. These things happen with monotonous frequency."

"What things?" Verity broke in, incensed.

"Boy meets girl," he said cruelly.

"You're impossible!"

"Yet knowledgeable. Peter meant every word he said . . . but only for the length of time he said it. Already, and I have no doubt about this, he has forgotten."

"You don't understand –" she endeavoured.

"No," he came in quietly, "*you* don't. You don't understand that Peter must be understood – and that only one woman ever has understood him yet, and it's not our mother, nor" . . . gently, that is if this man could be gentle . . . "you."

One woman. Dully Verity remembered what Bart had said previously. He had said: "Peter is already accounted for."

But – but by whom?

He broke in on her thoughts, gentle no longer. "Look, Miss Tyler, you're not hurt, you're not even remotely affected. Drop that injured guise."

"I wasn't aware I looked injured," she muttered.

"You didn't look the way you looked when you first came to the Castle."

"And how was that?"

There was a pause. It went on so long she began to wonder if he had heard her. Then he said: "Beautiful."

But he did not add to it, he did not explain it, so perhaps she only imagined it.

Presently he said, "I'll take you home."

"Thank you, no."

"Is that what you said to Peter?"

"I don't need to be taken home."

For answer he rose, crossed and paid the bill, led the way out of the restaurant. Without asking her, he opened the door of the car, and, not questioning his authority, she got in.

They drove in entire silence. Even when the bridge was open and they had to wait, they still did not speak. Verity looked down at the ship passing through the opened span up to Blackwattle Bay. She was thinking nothing at all; she seemed beyond thinking. She wondered what Bart Prince was thinking about, or whether he, too, was beyond thought.

As soon as the car stopped at her terrace, her hand went to the door. She must get out and inside the flat before he –

A hand covered hers, stopping any pressure on the catch.

"Why are you in such a hurry?"

"Please, Mr. Prince –"

"Please, Mr. Prince . . . is that what you gave Peter?"

"This is going too far," she said.

"On the contrary, it hasn't gone at all. Was it like that? Was it 'Please, Mr. Prince'?"

"No!" She fairly flung it at him.

"But it is to me?"

"You," she reminded him cruelly, not understanding her cruelty, not really believing she said it even after she had spoken it, "are not your brother."

It had immediate effect. She could see the old bitterness returning to him. His hand dropped away. He got out of his side of the car and came round and opened her door.

He said nothing but "Goodnight, Miss Tyler," then came back to his seat at the wheel. Before she reached her front door she heard the car draw away.

CHAPTER V

THE following day it seemed that Bart had spoken too quickly. In the afternoon's mail there was a letter from Melbourne for Verity.

Priscilla handed it to her without comment . . . Bart was out . . . and Verity took it also without speaking.

She held it for quite a while before she opened it. She waited for the quickening of the pulses that such a letter, Peter's letter, should bring. She wished desperately that she could summon up something – what sort of woman was she to change her heart so quickly as this? Yet had her heart ever been involved? Even without Bart's raw words to start all this, wouldn't she still have been asking herself this?

Clutching the letter, she crossed to the antique room, trying to stifle her feeling of guilt over Peter by anticipating what he wrote before she read it. It would be as his brother had said: Out of sight, out of mind. He might even have written an apology over the pleasant but unimportant dalliance, for that was all it had been, she knew it now, and she half-smiled. Though possibly if it was not an apology, it was an extrication. She smiled all the way now, thinking that yes, an extrication would be Peter Prince.

She took out the letter.

"My darling."

My darling. Verity tested Peter's opening uneasily. It didn't sound an apology, or even a bowing out. She realized with shame, shamed at her shallowness, that she had hoped it would be.

"My darling, Were you let down when I allowed my big brother Bart to browbeat me so mercilessly, banish me to Melbourne? Then if so, my sweet, I did it for you. (For myself, too. After years of indecision I have decided after all that trade is for me, especially since it involves you. That it has to be in another state is saddening, but I don't think it will be for long. Anyway, let's hope.)

"Verity, the magic is still working, so it must be the real thing. I've thought of no one else since I left you. Everywhere I look I see only your little face. That might not surprise you, not after what we came to realize about each other, but I must admit it rather has surprised me. I've never been the stable Prince. I'm sorry, dearest, but that is a fact, that is Peter. But now it is another tale. Write and tell me the same story from you, and until then I'll still look round and see only one face. (That's quite good, isn't it?) P."

She realized she held the letter so tightly that she was crumpling it. It would not matter, she would remember the words, if not with thrall, then certainly with triumph. Triumph against Bart Prince. Bart had been so confident, so sure, and he had been wrong. She put the letter in her pocket.

She took out her writing things that night to answer Peter. Yet what to say? The same story, as he had asked her, as his to her? She looked at the paper a long time, finding no words, then put the pen down again. Although it was rather late she decided she would visit Robin.

As she caught the bus she felt remiss about the last week, Peter's week, that had passed without her seeing her half-brother. She had disciplined herself after meeting Adele not to go to see Robin as often as she wanted, but these last days she had not wanted, because she had not even thought of Robin.

One thing, her brother had always been a night subject; he

69

would see nothing amiss in her turning up now at this hour.

As it happened it was Adele who opened the door, and for the first time the girl greeted her with less than her usually thinly-veiled animosity.

"I was wondering when you would come."

About to remind Adele that she could have contacted her herself, Verity said anxiously, "How's Robin?"

"Oh, he's all right. Not picking up, of course, that's right out, but it wasn't Rob I was worrying about. We had no remittance this month."

Verity turned her head away so that Adele would not see the dismay in her face. Before she had left London she had had a long talk with Mr. Carstairs, Robin's solicitor, and he had warned her that the money from the Ramsay estate that was being allotted to Robin could not last indefinitely. But he had not said it would be depleted this soon. Verity remembered sitting down in the Balmain flat after Robin's attack and going through figures, trying to approach the subject keenly and practically, not with a numbness in her heart. She had estimated that the money should see her brother out.

She glanced around at the lavish apartment. Obviously the way it was being spent it was not going to last, but even then it should still be forthcoming for a period at least.

"I'll see to it," she promised. "I'll write at once."

"That will take time, and right now we're down to our last cent. Really, I've never seen such mismanagement! That solicitor must be a fool. Why, without you we'd be stuck." Adele looked irritated.

Without you ... The meaning of the words came abruptly to Verity. Adele was obviously expecting her to ... she was relying on her for ...

She thought dully that ordinarily she would have rushed the chance to help Robbie, she would have made a jealous privilege of it, but at this present moment all she possessed was in the handbag under her arm, and though quite sufficient for herself, in fact generous, by Robin's and Adele's standards it would not be worth the taking. But she was wrong, for Adele said, "Anything will do until the cheque comes through. And see you don't forget to jerk that lawyer." She waited as Verity opened up the purse, then coolly accepted the entire contents.

Hiding her dismay, for she had only been paid that day, Verity allowed Adele gather up the notes. She did a quick mental arithmetic as Robin's wife pocketed the money briskly, saying, "Rob's asleep . . . he has these sedation things . . . you can look in on him, though, if you like." Her arithmetic told her that it was fortunate that she had paid the rent ahead, also bought her ferry tokens, but as for food . . .

Yet when she looked down on Robin, she forgot her own living in Robbie's now apparent less-than-living. Couldn't Adele see that this was no sedation but progressive slackening on her husband's frail grip of life?

Kissing him gently, she went out again.

In the flat she analysed her position. She had not accrued even one cent yet in her job, she had not been able to build up any supplies. Well, not to worry. Priscilla, she knew, would forward her some of her wages in advance. She sat down at once and wrote to Mr. Carstairs. She knew he would tell her the position honestly, how far the money had gone down, how long it could hold out. Then ruefully telling herself she would not have minded some of that meal that Bart had pushed away so uncaringly last night, she went to bed.

The next morning she arrived before Priscilla. At ten o'clock the secretary was still not there.

At noon Bart came in, asking Verity if she was inconvenienced without Cilla – had the phone been worrying her when she had a customer?

71

"Fortunately business has been rather quiet, so I was able to cope. Where is Priscilla?"

"Laid low," he told her.

"She's sick?"

"Quite, according to report."

"Oh." It was a blow. Verity had intended to ask Priscilla today. Well, there was always the Castle's tea or coffee and biscuits to eke her out until tomorrow, and at least her rent and fares were prepaid.

"Looks like you'll be coping for a while," Bart said a little anxiously. "The doc has forbidden her work for ten days."

"Ten days!" exclaimed Verity.

"Look, I'll be around." He took her dismay as concern for her ability to manage the business.

"Yes, I know." She tried to hide a note in her voice she felt sure must be as obvious as a shout, the note of panic at living on a handful of coins and raidings from a tin of biscuits for ten days.

For she would never ask from Bart.

She had no groceries in the flat – very unhousewife-like, but she had not been employed long enough yet to collect a supply. She was thinking this as she went home that night. In her bag were some of Priscilla's office biscuits. They had to eke her out for tea and breakfast. She wondered if Bart Prince kept as seeing an eye on the domestic side of the Castle as he did on the business side ... and the emotional. If he did, she was going to have some awkward explaining to do, for it was a funny thing, she half smiled whimsically, how, like A. A. Milne's bear who had helped himself to ham, jam, plum and pear, that the more you ate the less was there. In this instance, biscuits. She knew she could tell Priscilla later, receive a smile in response, but if Bart Prince kept a petty cash record it was going to be hard.

72

The first few days the biscuits kept her going, not very satisfactorily, but she felt little the worse. Then, while she was busy on a rather demanding customer one afternoon, Bart made the coffee instead.

"The bix are going down," he remarked casually. It was an innocent statement, probably meaning nothing at all, but Verity shrivelled sensitively, finding something implied in it. She was being foolish, her common sense told her that, but that night she took home no biscuits. She went to bed without any sustenance, went to work again the next morning still fasting. She was so hungry at morning tea-time she knew that if she started she probably would finish up the tin's entire contents. So she did not eat at all.

It wasn't until late afternoon that she found herself feeling weak and giddy. Whenever Bart was not around, she sat down and closed her eyes.

She had not long to go now. Bart had said casually earlier that Priscilla had phoned to say that she had made a quicker recovery than her doctor had anticipated, and would be back tomorrow. Verity felt she could last till tomorrow. She *must*.

Like all fainting attacks, later she could not have said at what precise moment this one occurred. At one moment she was sitting conserving herself, relaxing to try to help herself, to dispel her giddiness, the next moment she was prone and unaware on the floor. She had no memory of anything occurring, no feeling of consciousness returning. All she knew when she fluttered her eyes open again was Bart Prince wavering before her, his face gradually becoming steadier, then at last keeping still.

"Do you feel better now?" he asked.

"Yes, thank you."

"Are you prone to spells like this?"

"No."

"Then what brought this one about?" he asked forcefully, probingly, and she remembered his mother saying that he had begun a medical career.

"I don't know."

"Oh, come, you can do better than that."

"A virus of some sort, I expect. I – probably caught it from Priscilla."

"*Her* complaint is an old ankle injury," he said drily. He waited. "Have you any other symptoms? A chill? A headache?"

"No."

"Then have you eaten?" He asked it so sharply, so pertinently, so unexpectedly that she knew for all her pallor that her cheeks were reddening.

"Ah," he said.

He lifted more than helped her up, then he went and closed the doors of the Castle.

"Mr. Prince –" she objected, for it was not yet closing time, but he made a dismissive gesture with his hands and left her.

He came back almost at once, at least in her depletion it seemed at once, but in that brief time he had made strong sweetened coffee. He also had put biscuits at the side of it, the biscuits that today she had not touched.

Verity tried not to eat eagerly. He must never know the position she had got herself into. But there was no deceiving this man, she thought ruefully. Watching her keenly, he said: "So that's why the biscuit supply has been going down."

"No . . . I mean . . . that is –"

"What is it? A slimming project?"

"No."

"Some health project, then?"

"You really are mistaken, Mr. Prince, there's nothing at all."

"Look, I may not be the doctor of the family, but I still got myself up to the stage of knowing when someone is suffering from depletion. In other words, when they're hungry," he said sharply.

There was no arguing with him – anyway, she did not have the strength. She did not have the strength either to sit and hear his tirade, but that, she heard thankfully, was not to be. He had got up and left her. She heard his steps in the next room, that slightly dragging gait that marked Bart.

After that there was silence for a while.

Then he returned, and there was a noise she could not recognize and was too listless to try to recognize. It came from the office. Then he came back to where she still sat, and, without any preliminary words picked her up bodily and carried her to the office, to a seat at a cleared desk. There he had set a table. When he had gone away it must have been to buy food. With it he had hired the necessary plates and cutlery. He had even brought two napkins.

"We cut short our meal the other night," he said. "Now let's make amends."

For a few moments she felt stiff and awkward, and then hunger took over. With cheeks red with embarrassment, Verity ate ravenously.

To spare her, she suspected, he ate, too. The main course over, he poured a hearty red wine and produced a cheese. Later he brewed more coffee.

Only then did he lean across to her, and she wondered what it was he would say.

He said: "Before you explain, which I fully intend you to, let me tell you that if you ever do this again, young woman, you'll answer to me. Is that understood?"

"Yes," accepted Verity.

He had lit himself a cigarette.

"All right," he said, "why?" When she did not answer, he prompted, "You're sitting there until you tell me, Miss Tyler."

"I overspent myself," she said with a rush.

His brows raised. "But weren't you paid recently?"

"It happened that day," she confessed with pretended shame.

"So you're a spendthrift," he nodded. It seemed to amuse him, and she was willing for him to be amused with her, until his smile suddenly stopped and he said, "Now start again, and don't lie."

"It's not a lie. I didn't have any money. I'd paid my rent and I'd pre-purchased my ferry tokens, but I had no money. I didn't worry, because I knew Priscilla would advance me some, but Priscilla wasn't here and – and –"

"And you wouldn't ask me?"

"No."

"How long did all this last?"

"Not long."

"Priscilla went off last Tuesday. Was it that long?"

"Well – yes."

"You damn little fool," he said.

There was silence. She could see from the whitened knuckle bones of his long thin hands that he was angry, that he was trying to keep the anger in check.

"What did you find that was so important that you had to buy it at once?" he demanded at last.

"I . . . well . . ." she stammered.

"Yes?"

"It wasn't like that."

"I'll believe that. Because you didn't buy anything, did you, you gave something away."

"No. No – I didn't. I –"

"Don't lie. You gave it to your brother."

"No."

"Then to Dellie."

She tried to fabricate, she didn't want this man in this, but she could not find the words.

"I know," he continued, "because Adele also spoke to me."

"Spoke to you?" she gasped.

"Why not? I told you we were old acquaintances."

"She spoke to you – regarding money?"

"Regarding it only. She didn't ask for it. She was very concerned, because nothing had come through. It's a pity" ... he said coldly ... "that that pair were not left to manage their own affairs without having to ask you to act for them."

"If you mean I'm doling out their money, you're very, very wrong. I wasn't aware that they were in the position they are until Adele told me. I – I wrote to the solicitor at once."

He shrugged meanly at that. "As I said, managing their affairs."

She decided to pass that. She said stiffly, "I'm sorry Adele bothered you. She should have come to me."

"She did." A thin reminding smile.

"But to you, too."

"I'm not blaming her, when a certain standard of living has been enjoyed it's hard to accept anything less. Besides" ... deliberately ... "you hadn't been to see them for some time to *know* their position." He left it at that, but Verity knew he was telling her silently what that time had comprised. It had been her Peter episode.

"Well, enough of that," he said presently. "You say you've written to England?"

"Yes."

"Good. But until the matter is fixed up, we must not, of

course, have a repetition of this." He made a gesture to the table.

"I'll clear up," she began childishly, pretending it was the office disarray he was decrying, but she was stopped by his angry frown.

"You know what I mean, Miss Tyler, you know I refer to this stupid starvation of yours. You must give me a promise now that you'll never do this again."

"And if I don't give it?"

"Then we spend the night here. After all, we have plenty of beds." Now he gave a maddening smile.

Verity looked down. "I know you mean well," she said at last, "but – well, none of this is your affair."

"Fainting on my floor is my affair, causing me to close early is my affair!" he snapped.

"Always business."

"Why not?" A small significant pause. "What else is there? But there, I do it again, that self-pity. Please consider it unsaid. And to ease your mind until this remittance detail is adjusted, you must accept this sum to give to your brother."

"No!"

"Have no fears, it will be deducted from your salary," he answered her.

"No."

"Then I'll have to offer it to Dellie myself."

"*No*." This time Verity spoke with distress.

"Please yourself," he shrugged.

"You're sure you'll record this loan?" she insisted.

"Just you try to get out of it."

"Then – thank you," she said.

She watched him as he rose and went to a desk, unlocked it and took out some notes. When he came back he did not hand them to her at once. He sat down and flicked them through his long fingers, not counting them, just flicking them. His eyes held hers. At length he pushed them over.

"There's a separate bundle," he said drily, "for yourself. Don't give that to the Ramsays as well and so repeat this performance, or I mightn't be as tolerant as I am today."

"Tolerant?" She said faintly.

"Tolerant. Then it would really be a case of 'Please, Mr. Prince.'"

He sat back and watched her go.

CHAPTER VI

IN the week that followed Verity had the embarrassment, if not the personal pang, of seeing everything that Bart had said of Peter eventuate.

As each letter arrived there was a progressive diminishing of Peter's warm interest in her. From the second letter, which still declared that he "saw her face wherever he looked" but no longer talked of any "magic", the correspondence went on, until, with the latest letter, "seeing her" went the same lost way as the "magic."

Relieved, yet still rankling because of Bart's unerring pre-knowledge, Verity accepted the episode as just one of those things, particularly when the correspondence stopped, only to renew itself with no mention at all of her but a thinly-concealed excitement in a brand-new interest – Cassandra.

"Talk of coincidences," wrote Peter, "in this bustling city where surely the only way to meet anyone is by rendezvous, I have (at last) encountered the illustrious Cassandra. I say at last because I had heard so much of her. Remember, Verity, I believed you were her.

"It was unplanned, as I said. I caught my thumb in a car door ... no, no damage ... and was taken to an outpatients department. Who should deal with me there but Cassandra? Oh, what a girl!"

Then came another letter.

"You have met Cassandra, haven't you? The Prince legend

is that she's for Matthew, but, as Cassandra has pointed out, not that you would notice. My eldest brother must be a damn fool. She's glorious.

"She's as pleased as I am for us to be getting around together. I think that lovely girl is a bit confused with her world, and I intend to spare her any more confusion."

Later that week there was a further letter.

"Verity, I really have fallen for Cassandra. I've never felt like this before in all my life, and I'm certain she's feeling the same about me. It's just too bad for old Matthew, but anyone who would hold up a girl like Cass doesn't need any sympathy. As for me, I'm a free agent." – Oh, Peter!

"Anyway, old girl, I wanted you to know." – Old girl!

"Old girl." It was Priscilla, and she was standing at the door; she was watching Verity reading the letter, and she was wearing an enigmatical smile.

Caught out, Verity folded the letter and said, "You seem to know the drill."

"It's always the same with Peter," Priscilla said, and her tone conveyed nothing at all. "One attack follows the other. It chronic. I'm sorry if you're hurt, Verity, but somehow I don't think you really are."

"Not hurt," Verity confirmed, and waited.

After a few moments, Priscilla said, "One day there'll be no more of this. Peter will be different. He'll settle." There was a note in the secretary's voice that Verity could not quite place. Several times Priscilla had puzzled her with her concern for Peter. It had seemed more than the usual sisterly concern, since sister to Peter was what Priscilla would be on that day when Bart overcame whatever it was that stopped him now and instead married his Cilla, for at no time had Verity credited Bart's statement that he alone of the Princes remained not yet accounted for.

"Was it –" Priscilla paused. "Was it just a falling out once more that Peter wrote about?" Now there was a slightly strained note in her voice, a frown on her serene brow.

"No. A new face for Peter – Cassandra's."

"Cassandra?" Priscilla, who had turned to leave, whipped round again. Now she looked really upset. "Of course ... they're both in Melbourne," she recalled, "but how –"

"Peter had an accident. No" ... as Priscilla stepped quickly forward ... "only a minor one. It was Cassandra who attended him."

A few moments went by, then Priscilla said flatly, "Yes, that's just what would happen. Peter draws pretty girls to him like a magnet. But Cassandra isn't just pretty, she's –"

"Glorious," said Verity for her. She added: "Peter's words."

Mr. Carstairs had not replied to Verity as promptly as she had thought he would. She knew the solicitor well, and had expected he would write at once, perhaps cable. However, no news was good news, and when an answer did come, it would probably be an assurance that some minor detail had held the money up.

But when Verity saw the bulky air letter the following evening after work, she knew that the solicitor's time in replying had been because he had been taking the trouble to account in detail to her. And, as she flicked through the sheets reporting the different expenditures to see the final figure, the sum total was anything but good.

She went out that night to Robin's flat. Robin was up and at first glance seemed a little better. But Verity, experienced now, looked to the dulled eyes, the lacklustre general tone.

"What's got into Carstairs, V?" Robin complained testily. "The cheque was right down this time."

"Oh, you got one, then?"

82

"You didn't think," cut in Adele, "that we were still living on what you handed out?"

Robin looked upset over that, but years of only bothering about himself made his concern transitory.

"Write to him again, will you, Sis, explain to him what a foul run I've had, how I can't be put around like this. I'd do it myself, only I just can't seem to concentrate lately. Another aftermath, I suppose."

"And until we get satisfaction," said Adele, "can you –"

"Yes," said Verity, and handed across the notes that Bart had given her.

She left soon after that. She felt very disturbed.

She was glad that the work at the Castle completely absorbed her. Without it, she would have had time to brood, to worry herself more than she had time to worry now. She was glad, too, when Bart announced the winning of a contract to decorate the whole of a new multi-storey government building, adding that not only would he be away for a week to assess the situation but that he would require Priscilla for note-taking.

"Can you cope?" he asked Verity.

"I did before."

"With rather dire results," he reminded her thinly.

"This time," she said boldly, "I'll see that the biscuit tin is full to the brim."

"This time," he amended, "if I return to find a situation like before I'll –"

"Yes?"

"Just practise your plea for mercy," he advised shortly "your 'Please, Mr. Prince.'"

"You never forget anything, do you, Mr. Prince?"

There was a silence. It grew to such a long silence that Verity looked at him uneasily. With an effort he seemed to bring himself back from something that tortured him.

"I wish to heaven I could!" It was more a cry, Verity thought.

He had tight control of himself, though. At once he went briefly through some of the stock with her, telling her what he wanted pushing. "I need space," he explained, "I'm expecting a new consignment. We don't exactly run sales, but I leave it to you to find a price suitable to all to get rid of an article. You'll be pushed, what with the urgent correspondence, but anything else can wait for Cilla, and the phone as well as the shop. In which case . . ." He paused a moment, looking at her. Then he said, "I want you to have this."

She looked at notes he was handing her in surprise, then she shook her head. "You already pay me generously."

"For one job. I don't ask anyone to do two jobs for the price of one."

"Mr. Prince" . . . they never called each other by their names now . . . "there is also the money you've already advanced me."

"Loans, and don't fret, as such they're safely down in my little black book. This is entirely different. This is business. I'm paying you for a job I expect to be well done."

"It will be," she gratefully assured him.

She got into the practice of arriving earlier in the morning and going through the mail. In that way she was free to concentrate on her own domain for the other working hours. It proved a good idea, for though there was much that only Priscilla could handle, there were also quite a number of inquiries that needed to be dealt with at once. It also, or so, taken by surprise, she thought at first, put her into the position of apprehending a thief.

Except . . . and one glance assured her of this . . . he was *not*. When Mrs. Prince had had her three sons, if they were not identical there was still an unmistakably close resemblance between them. Peter, for instance, was a more suave Bart, yet Peter, looking across at her "thief", was not so outstanding as this Prince. Noting his added maturity, Verity knew he must be Matthew Prince. The first Prince. The eldest. The gracious prince of the old fairytale. The one, Bart had said, earmarked for Cassandra . . . though by recent developments –

She went forward to where Matthew Prince was letting himself into the store with a personal key and held out her hand.

"Mr. Prince," she greeted him.

"You haven't added 'of course'," he smiled at Verity, "people usually do."

"Of course," she obliged.

"Yes, I am Matthew Prince. I'm sorry if I alarmed you, but there was something I needed from here, and I thought if I called early –"

"I've also been calling early," Verity told him. "Your brother has won a big contract for the Castle and has taken Priscilla to help him with it for the week, leaving me, the newcomer, to hold the fort."

"Which I have no doubt you do admirably," he said sincerely, his eyes estimating and approving her at the same time.

"Thank you. I try." Verity paused. "Can I help you find what you came fo?"

He frowned slightly. "I hope so." He got into step beside Verity and they went down the corridor. "I want Cassie's address. I rang her flat, but there's no reply. I think" . . . deepening of the frown . . . "she may have gone away. Have you met Cassandra?"

"Yes."

"Then –?"

"You didn't know she had left Sydney temporarily?" Verity asked tactfully.

"I know nothing, except that she doesn't answer me when I phone."

"Cassandra ... I met her briefly before she went ... has gone to Melbourne. She has taken a relief position in a hospital there."

"Do you know which hospital?"

"No ... but your brother would," Verity said unthinkingly.

"My brother," said Matthew Prince quickly. "You mean –"

"I mean both, actually, for Bart would have the name, but really I was referring to Peter."

"Peter," Matthew said after her. "Peter," he said again. There was a pause. "So Peter would know, would he?" He gave a slight shrug.

She told him briefly about Peter's mishap. He nodded as she related it, then when she had finished he said, "It doesn't help much, does it?"

"No. I'm sorry."

He turned and smiled warmly at Verity. "Why should you be sorry? You told me all you know."

Something made her say impulsively, ". . . Sorry for you."

"Meaning?"

"What you meant when you shrugged like you did just now."

"You mean – our one and only Peter?"

"The charming prince," she nodded. She told him quickly about the old fairytale. She found him very easy to talk to.

"Well, I don't know," he said after she had finished. "I don't know if I was ever the gracious prince. Conscientious, perhaps, which is after all often a word for dull, or so I'm told by Cassie."

"I don't find you dull," said Verity.

Now he looked at her thoughtfully. "Do you know what," he said presently, "I don't believe you do. Look, I'm due at the

86

hospital. After that I've surgery. I have my own practice now, you know. Then there's home calls. However, *you* won't get away early, either, will you?"

"No—"

"Then—dinner?"

"I don't know. You see, I've already dined with two of the three Princes, and it could seem like I'm making a habit of it."

"But one couldn't be left out," he pleaded. As she still hesitated he said, "Please," and she found she could not resist the quiet appeal.

"I could be closed up and ready by eight," she agreed.

"That will be wonderful."

The day dragged, though of late she seemed barely to have arrived before it was time to close up and go; Verity had supposed it was because she was busy that the hours had flown. But today she was just as busy, yet the hours passed slowly. She realized with a little rueful smile that it was because she was having dinner with Matthew Prince. She had not been out for a while now, and the diversion appealed to her. — Matthew appealed.

He was at the Castle on time, a little tired-looking, and she supposed he had had a heavy day. She suggested coffee before they left, and he agreed eagerly, sitting back in Priscilla's chair as she brewed it, closing his eyes.

"We needn't go," she proffered gently.

"Of course we must go."

"There's a place not far up the avenue. I could bring something back."

He looked at her eagerly, but wiped the look off at once. "What kind of escort would you think me?"

"A nice one." He really was tired, there was a fatigue line from his eyes to his mouth. "Please, Mr. Prince —" Please, Mr. Prince, that was Bart's gibe.

"Matthew, Verity."

"Please, Matthew, you're obviously not up to the social graces tonight. Frankly, after a day coping by myself in this store, I don't think I am, either. Why don't we just relax and talk here? I mean, after we've had something to eat."

"It sounds attractive," he admitted wistfully, "I do feel I've met as many people as I want today, present company excluded. On the other hand it also sounds terribly mean."

"I don't know why," she laughed, "you'll be paying. Look, why not come with me and choose? It's only a few doors up."

He jumped up eagerly, enthusiasm making him seem much younger. "I haven't done anything like this for ages. Lead on, Verity."

The shop from which Bart had bought the supplies that night of Verity's hunger faint was a very attractive one. Paper carrier bags were produced by the obliging shopkeeper, and Matthew and Verity had a lot of fun choosing their take-away meal. Matthew insisted that although they were not dining out they must still go through the courses, and he not only ordered appetisers, soup, entrée and an elaborate sweet, but white wine as well.

"This is fun," he said, adding little white onions and red peppers to his purchases, "this is as much fun as I've had in a long time."

"Your fault?" Verity asked carefully.

"Why do you say that?"

"Having fun is usually your own thing," she said. "At the very least you have to make the effort."

"I've never been what you might call a funny fellow," he admitted. "I'm afraid I'm a bit of a sobersides."

"The fairytale said gracious," she smiled.

"Oh, that fairytale!"

They were walking back to the Castle now, both carrying

bags, occasionally their hands brushing. When they got to the office, Verity set the desk as Bart had set it that night – except that she had forgotten to pick up the paper plates.

"Oh, dear!" She looked rueful and nodded to her omission. "I'll go back."

"I'll go. No, neither of us will. You've brought the implements. What else do two people need when they like each other?" He smiled warmly as he said that "When they like each other."

Eating from one dish necessitated sitting close. They sat close. When they had finished, when the wine was finished, there seemed no reason to sit apart again. A comfortable silence encompassed them, for quite a while neither spoke.

When Matthew broke the silence at last it was tentatively, a little hesitantly, but only because of what he spoke about, not because he was saying it to Verity. Verity had the feeling that he was completely relaxed with her, as she was with him.

"So Cassie and Pete have met up at last?"

"Yes, according to Peter. But why did you say that?"

"At last?"

"Yes."

"Because I suppose in a way I've always tried to work it that they didn't meet."

"They had to, some time."

"I expect so, but Peter . . . well, if you know Peter . . ."

"I do know Peter." Her eyes met his a moment, then she smiled back ruefully to his own rueful smile. "The charming prince," she said. "Only" . . . a pause . . . "it doesn't last."

"But one day it could." Now it was Matthew who paused. "This time it could."

"Then why, Matthew, why? Oh, do please forgive the intrusion, but why?"

"Why haven't I done something about it?"

"Yes."

"You mean – like tie Cassandra down?"

Verity nodded.

"Because I wasn't ready, or rather my prospects weren't. I've always had this thing about a man building up something for his wife, not just – just –"

"Cassandra didn't want you a raving success, no woman would."

"I know, I know. But –" He fell silent again.

They left the subject at that point, and talked about generalities, coming to the general practice he now had, and how he hoped to extend it.

"It's a new district and I'm the first doctor. It's a challenge." Presently he said, "I can't tell you how good I feel having talked to you like this. You've unloosened me. I think I must have needed you."

"And the picnic meal?"

"That, too. It was much better than going out. But I still owe you a proper meal, Verity. When?"

"That's entirely up to a G.P. An assistant to Woman's Castle hasn't the same demands made on her. A dropside table is never a matter of life or death."

"Surgery is at the same hours throughout the week. I have no imminent cases. Of course if an emergency arose –"

"I'd understand," she assured him.

"Then when?"

"Tomorrow night?" She flushed, thinking she might be hurrying things, but for obvious reasons, Bart reasons, she wanted to meet Matthew while his brother was away from the Castle, and already the week was halfway through.

She became aware that he was laughing at her. "Do you know when tomorrow is?"

"Why – tomorrow."

"Right, but I really think you mean tonight."

"Tonight?" She looked at him in disbelief, then checked her watch. He was right. Tomorrow was now tonight, it was after midnight. She had never known time to go so quickly.

"I must go," she said hastily.

"Or the carriage will turn into a pumpkin and you'll be back sitting among the cinders?"

She laughed at him. "I'm a working woman. I can't keep these late hours and give the Castle what I want to give it."

"I must go, too. I suppose I shouldn't have stopped so long, but I just couldn't call a halt."

"Then you knew the time?"

"Yes."

"And you didn't tell me?"

"No." A pause. "Verity – I was lonely."

I was lonely. Matthew's quiet admission rang in Verity's ears long after she had gone to bed. I was lonely. Well, he hadn't been tonight. She hadn't been. She thought how the time had flown and what a pleasant evening it had been with the eldest Prince. She knew he had enjoyed it as she had. She did not try to sleep, she just lay relaxed.

When morning came she had snatched only a few naps, and as she joined the rush into town she knew she would not look her best for her formal night out.

At six the phone went and it was Matthew.

"Verity?"

"Yes."

"All beautifully dressed and desirable?"

"Most unbeautiful and undesirable."

"I know you could be neither, but you sound as drained-out as I am, as – well, an unforward-looking."

"You're quite right, Matthew," she said.

"Then I wonder could we . . . I mean it's not fair of me to

ask, but I did appreciate it. Somehow it was like being home –"

"You mean do what we did last night?"

"Yes." Diffidently.

"Matthew, I'd love that." Eagerly.

"Then you enjoyed it, too?"

"Very much."

"Then you stay on at the Castle. I'll bring the food."

"And the plates?" she laughed.

There was a short silence at the other end.

"We got along all right last night without them."

Now it was Verity's turn to hesitate. But she didn't. She said at once, and warmly: "Oh, yes."

After two nights it had become a pattern. Verity would finish the day's work, close the shop, then while the percolator bubbled she would wash, take off her smock and comb her hair. By then Matthew would have arrived, smiling like a delighted small boy over the goodies he had in the carrier bag, pleased when he could show her something they had not sampled before.

That he found pleasure in their relaxed meals was very apparent. "After our father died and my mother had to carry on the business, we three boys were put into boarding school. I liked it all right, I've always been fairly adaptable ... rather dull, as I said before . . ."

"I would say adaptable."

"You're kind, Verity. Yes, I suffered no setbacks, but I do remember longing to sit at an unshared table."

"You're sitting at a shared one now."

"Not shared by thirty boys. Anyway, this is a desk, and yet –"

"And yet, Matthew?"

"It could be a family table in a home."

"It's a home," she reminded him, "and home's what a woman's castle is."

"Yes," he said quietly, and his eyes smiled into hers.

It was Verity who forced her glance away in the end. This won't do, she thought. Matthew and I are seeing far too much of each other: it means nothing, it *is* nothing, we're just two rather confused, rather lonely people who have turned to each other for company, for companionship . . . but it still won't do.

Yet when they parted that night and Matthew asked eagerly "Tomorrow?" she could not say no.

Occasionally during the day Bart called in to see how she was coping. He reported that he and Priscilla were progressing favourably with the assessment.

"It's going to be a bigger job than we thought. We may take longer. Is that all right with you?"

"Perfectly."

"You're sure?"

"Why the doubt? Isn't my work satisfactory?"

He frowned. "I didn't ask you that. Your work is quite satisfactory, so satisfactory I'm wondering if you are over-exerting yourself," he said probingly.

She *was* over-exerting herself. Though she would not have admitted it, there was always present an uneasy doubt, a reluctant knowledge that if Bart had frowned on her episode with Peter, he would more than frown on this. Though not fully aware of it, she had salved her conscience by putting more into Woman's Castle than she could have credited from herself. Bart had evidently noticed something. He was still looking at her searchingly.

"There's no prize at the end," he said briefly. "I require you only to cope, not create an all-time record."

"I'm only working normally," she assured him.

"I hope so. I also hope among other things that you are

93

keeping the regulation hours. Are you, Miss Tyler?"

A little nettled, she said, "What are the hours? Oh, I know Priscilla's are nine to five, but mine depend on other issues, don't they?"

There was a silence. Then Bart said, "Yes – other issues." He was still looking estimatingly at her.

Presently he said, "You look different."

"I assure you I'm the same."

"But what is the same?"

"What do you mean, Mr. Prince?"

There was another pause. He seemed about to say something, but he must have changed his mind.

"Everything seems as it should be, Miss Tyler," he said briskly. "We could wind up the assessment next week. Any queries before I go?"

"No."

"Any troubles?"

"No."

"In fact all plain sailing?"

"Yes, Mr. Prince. Thank you."

"On these records" ... he tapped the ledger ... "I should say gratefully to you to keep it up. – Whatever you're doing."

She waited ... but he did not say it. He gave her another long steady look, then left the shop.

She did not see him again until the end of the week. *But she saw Matthew.*

Verity and Doctor Prince were on much closer terms now. He had listened sympathetically to her account of Robin, nodding now and then, inserting pertinent questions. When she had answered them, and when she had finished her report, he had said gently: "There's nothing I can add, Verity, you must know that."

"Yes. I know that nothing can be done, nothing except to

94

keep him as contented and happy as possible." She was silent a while; she was wondering how long the money that went a long way if not the entire way to Robin's contentment and happiness could last. "Matthew . . ."

"Yes, my dear?" The dear was said kindly, with understanding.

"How – how long?"

"Can a doctor ever say that? He can estimate, but finally it's another authority. Also, the man's will enters into it, his capacity to hold on."

"Then – an estimate?"

A pause. "Not long," Matthew said.

Matthew also talked about himself.

"The moment I saw Cassandra, Verity, I knew . . . at least I *think* now I knew."

She looked quickly at him at that "think."

"What are you saying, Matthew?"

"I don't know. For the life of me I don't know. Except" . . . he hesitated . . . "except why, oh, why can't she understand? Understand how important my work is to me, how I must find my roots in my work first." He looked at Verity. "*You* understand."

"Yes, but I may be differently constructed from Cassandra. I may not have another capacity that she has."

"Capacity for what?" he asked a little harshly, and in his harshness he reminded her more of Bart Prince than Peter, whom she had judged he most resembled before.

"Capacity for love?" she suggested . . . then she found herself meeting Matthew's eyes, and flushing vividly.

For a long time he said nothing, he just sat looking back at her, looking deeply. Then he rose and sighed. "Tomorrow is another day, little one." There was an infinite gentleness in that "little one."

There had been no more letters from Peter, and Verity had expected none. Unlike Priscilla, who had said of the third Prince's talent for collecting, and discarding, lovely girls a bleak "But *Cassandra* —" Verity had at no time anticipated anything else than the same as had been meted out to her.

She was wrong.

"Verity, be the first to know —" said the letter from Peter that came the following morning. Verity read it to the end, then put it down. Poor Matthew, she thought.

She would never have told the doctor had he not probed it out of her.

"Matthew, do you delve professionally as you're delving now?" she complained at length.

"Of course. I must." He paused. "You *have* had something from Peter, haven't you?"

"Yes."

"What does he say?"

"Oh, Matthew!" she sighed.

"All right then, just tell me one thing: Is it going the same way as it went with you, with the rest? Here today, gone to-morrow?"

She sat silent.

"Answer me, Verity."

"No, it's not going the same way."

"Then Peter and Cassandra —"

"Yes. I'm sorry, Matthew."

There was a dead silence. For quite a long time Verity could not bring herself to look up at Matthew. But when she did his first words to her completely surprised her. For Matthew said quite calmly, without any heroics, without any anger against anyone . . . with only emotion for her:

"Come away with me, Verity."

CHAPTER VII

"YOU'RE not serious, Matthew!" Verity looked back at him in disbelief. This could not be Doctor Prince, the first Prince. The "gracious prince."

"I think," Matthew said slowly, deliberately, "I've never been more serious in all my life."

"It's rebound. It has to be. You're hurt. You're lost. You're turning to someone, anyone at all, and it just happens to be me."

"Perhaps it could be rebound, Verity, but I can truthfully tell you that in this moment it doesn't seem like that at all. Instead . . . well, instead it seems the most wonderful moment in my life. It seems –" He took her hand in his strong surgeon hand. "It seems –" He paused. "Also," he went on presently, unable to finish what he had begun, "I don't feel hurt at all – indeed, I don't think I *feel* anything at all, except –"

"Except a numbness," she hazarded.

"Except a gratefulness to you," he corrected stubbornly.

"Gratefulness isn't enough."

"It's a start, everything has to have a start."

"And with anyone?"

"With you." Now he said it intentionally.

"Matthew –" she began.

"Oh, I know how this sounds to you, Verity, and I know it should sound like that, too, to me. But it still doesn't. This last week has been the happiest week of my life."

"Happiness," said Verity with a wisdom she did not know she possessed, "has to include more than we happen to have. Real happiness, the kind I believe you're talking about" ... she flushed ... "can't be built on just companionable happiness as we have known it, it has to go much deeper than that, it has to – well, it has to –" But her wisdom left her, and, as they had with him, the words ran out.

"I don't know about all that," said Matthew a little wearily. "I only know I've been able to talk with you as I've never talked to Cassie."

"Has Cassandra been able to talk to *you*?" probed Verity fairly.

"Two people should meet halfway," he said doggedly. "I talked to you, you listened to me, you talked to me, I listened to you."

"Did you ever listen to Cassandra?"

He grew silent.

"*Did* you, Matthew?" Verity persisted.

He answered, "Cassie never listened to me."

They were getting nowhere, nowhere on the subject of Cassandra, too deep on the subject of Matthew Prince and Verity Tyler.

"Matthew, go home now," Verity said. For a moment she thought he was going to refuse, then he smiled ruefully at her, kissed her cheek, then left.

Verity tidied up, then left, too. As she went down the street she wondered ... but was afraid to wonder too deeply ... what tomorrow would bring.

It brought Bart.

He was dragging his leg a little as he did when he was tired, but he wore that satisfied look of a job going well.

"Everything's falling into place," he told Verity, "a few hitches here and there, but nothing really for an assignment of this size."

"I'm glad."

"You mightn't be," he shrugged. "Although we're progressing favourably Cilla now believes it will take even longer than the extra time I warned you. In other words, Miss Tyler, you'll be asked to cope another week."

"That's all right," she said.

He looked at her shrewdly. "Very confident, aren't you?"

"What do you want?" she came back, irritated. "A defeated attitude? A doubt if I can keep on?"

"No, I like assurance as much as the rest. Only . . ." He was looking at her curiously now.

"Yes, Mr. Prince?"

"You seem different somehow."

"You said that last time."

"I say it again. You *are* different."

"Then that should please you."

"Also," he said, ignoring her comment, "you seem *very* eager to continue here by yourself." As she did not speak, he asked sharply, "Which you are, Miss Tyler?"

He was silent for a while. Then: "Has my brother been around?"

She caught her breath, but in that breath he continued, "Because if Peter has chucked this Melbourne tour he'll have to answer for it."

"No," she came in smoothly, "he hasn't been around."

As he went through the records of her sales, the copies of any correspondence she had thought should be answered, he said casually, "If Matthew comes in, see to it that he gets Cassandra's address. I'll leave it with you. He doesn't deserve it, playing hard to get with a girl like that, but I like to be Cupid. Besides, with Peter in the same city, one never knows." – So he hadn't learned yet, Verity thought. The thought was pushed aside as Bart, glancing up at her, asked: "Has Matthew been in by any chance?"

"Yes. He's very like you. I mean you're like him, except—"

"All the Princes are alike," Bart drawled. "*Except.*" He gave that old bitter derogatory laugh, but he did not add the usual bitter comment. As Verity did not speak, he went on: "My dear mamma evidently knew only the one pattern. To give her her due, she had variations, or should it be a standard? Mediocre, better, best. You can allot the grades." As she still did not speak, he got up and moved towards the door. "Don't forget about Matthew."

"I won't."

How could she? Verity thought.

Sitting in her favourite position at the flat window last night, she had analysed, or tried to analyse, herself. It hadn't been easy. She had never been the sort of person that she was uncomfortably aware she must seem now. For instance one week Peter. Then soon after, *much too soon*: Matthew. She had wondered at the difference in herself, for she always had been a very stable girl. As a child, her mother had said that once Verity had a friend she had her for ever.

She could not understand it . . . nor could she understand the undercurrents and the crosscurrents and the too swift currents that seemed to be upsetting the previously quiet flow of her life. Almost, she thought, as if a major change had taken place in her.

Matthew did not contact her for several days, and in her uncertainty she was glad of that.

Then he rang . . . and she felt her concern going out to him as he said sensitively: "Verity? Verity, my dear, I'm sorry."

"That's all right, Matthew." She did not ask "Sorry for

100

what?" because she felt she knew already, she knew that he never really had meant that "Verity, come away with me." Never Matthew. She said so now, hoping it would help him.

"But I did mean it," he said at once, "that is I meant –"

"Matthew" . . . gently . . . "what did you mean?"

A silence at the other end, then, wretchedly: "I just don't know."

He told her he was working hard. He would not see her for several more days.

"I think that would be a good thing," she agreed. She related his brother's instruction to pass Cassandra's address on to him. When this was met with silence, and the silence grew, she called, "Did you hear me, Matthew?"

"Yes, I heard. But don't bother about the address."

"What do you mean, Matthew?"

"I'll ring on Thursday, V."

There was still no letter from Mr. Carstairs telling Verity how Robin now stood, and it was with trepidation that Verity visited Robin and Adele again; she would not know what to answer to Adele if she questioned her as to what held up the cheque.

As it happened Adele was in such a good mood that Verity knew some moments of doubt. Robin was a spender; she knew Adele would be the same; and the amount she had given Adele, though large by her own standards, would not have satisfied that pair for this long. Instantly her mind jumped to Bart, and she felt herself withdrawing in distaste at the thought of what Adele could have tried, and, from the look of her, could have succeeded in.

She could not ask, but she learned, anyway, without asking.

As she was leaving she made a complimentary remark on Adele's new dress. She had left Robin in the lounge. The two girls stood at the flat door.

"Not bad," acknowledged Adele.

"A Sydney make?"

"You could say" . . . a little laugh . . . "that it was locally inspired in every way." There was no mistaking Adele's emphasis, but in case Verity did mistake it, Adele said, "Bart is a dear."

"Bart!" It was out before Verity could stop it, dismay with it.

Adele pounced triumphantly on the dismay. "Why not? I knew Bart Prince a long time before you did. Yes" . . . another little laugh . . . "we knew each other *very well*."

Sickened, Verity turned and went down the apartment stairs.

But the next day what Adele had said was lost in a worry she had known she must face soon, but had not anticipated as soon as this. The answer came from Mr. Carstairs, and the news could not have been worse. There was nothing remaining, nothing at all, of the Ramsay estate.

"I have delayed my reply to you, Verity" . . . Mr. Carstairs was an old family friend . . . "for the reason that I have been exhausting every possible channel. I know how important it is" . . . Verity had told him of Robin's prognosis . . . "and I only wish my news could be more favourable."

There followed a detailed account, of which Verity took small notice. She had implicit trust in the solicitor . . . she even suspected that final debt written down did not include the fee that his services should entail.

She was shocked. She had not expected anything as bad as this. She did not know what she would do. It had been all right to make a vow that Robin would never be told, but when she had made it there had been something, very little admittedly, but something. Now there was only a debt. Debts had to be paid. But how? How?

She yearned to talk to someone, to confide in them, to be advised. If only Adele had been the right kind of wife, a wife she could have gone to and told the whole unfortunate story. But the right kind of wife would not have been interested in the story, only concerned with Robin, and Robin's health.

There must be someone, Verity despaired.

Almost as if in answer, the telephone pealed. As she picked it up mechanically, still wrapped in her abject thoughts, Matthew's voice came over the wire ... and at once she felt cut loose from her forebodings. They were still there, of course, but Matthew's contact seemed to help her. She remembered reading once where a change of pain is almost as miraculous as a cessation of pain. Now Matthew with his own troubles seemed to help her with hers.

"Verity."

"Matthew."

"I said I'd ring."

"Yes."

"To say" ... but a little smile somewhere now ... "will you come away with me?"

"Matthew, not that again?"

"No, my dear, not that again. V, I'm sorry to the ends of the world. Of course I didn't mean it. You knew, didn't you, you sensed all the time that it was still Cassie with me, always was, always has been, is, always will be."

"Yes, Matthew, I sensed that."

"And for that reason I want you to come away with me."

"Matthew, are you mad?" she gasped.

"Hear me out, V, I'm not playing tit for tat, anything like that. I'm just flying down to Melbourne to put my cards on the table, to tell Cassie that she was right, that I was wrong, that building a career is very good, but that love comes first."

"Oh, Matthew, that's wonderful!"

"But only if you come, too. To lend me courage, to prod me. I'm a dull stick, I told you that. Most of all, if it is called for, I need you to take Peter out of the picture."

"Oh, Matthew, none of that is necessary. You should be able to handle it all yourself."

"Should, yes, but don't forget what I am."

"A good doctor."

"And a rotten executive. Verity, please come. I need your help."

"But, Matthew, it wouldn't be ... well, right." She had been thinking of Bart as she answered this, Bart who had said something of the sort, tongue in cheek probably, but still he had said it.

"Melbourne is all of an hour's flying time," said Matthew drily. "We would be back the same day." For a few moments Verity was silent.

"It's still impossible," she reminded him. "The store has to open."

"But it will be closed all of next week-end – it's a public holiday, even women's castles close up. Only hardworked doctors remain on deck, but I've snared myself the services of a good locum."

Again she was silent. It would be a break, she thought eagerly, and with Robin's troubles heavy on her shoulders she felt she needed a break. Besides, in her backing of Matthew, or so he had said, she certainly would be talking to him, he would be talking back to her. Talk, she yearned. Someone to spill things to.

"Verity?" came Matthew's voice, anxious, pleading. Poor Matthew, he really did need someone to nudge him on, she half-smiled.

But still something stopped her from answering ... yet not

104

something, she knew intrinsically, but some*one*. Bart. How would Bart take to this?

But need Bart know? Matthew saw very little of his brother. They were on excellent terms, but not the terms that would entail Matthew ringing Bart to say: "I took your assistant down with me to Melbourne."

It came down finally to a matter of conscience, everything came down eventually to that, and her conscience, Verity told herself, was clear. – It also came down to human contact, which in her present state she knew she must have ... and to the contributing fact that when it came to human contact, Matthew offered all the sympathy and comfort she could need. He was a sympathetic and comforting person, not like –

"Verity?"

"Yes, Matthew," she said, "I'll come."

The doctor called round just after closing time. He did not bring the carrier bags of goodies, that phase was over. But it had benefited both of them, Verity thought.

He waited long enough, though, for a coffee, telling her his arrangements as they drank together.

"I'm hurrying back now, V. Bryan, my locum, is calling round, and I want to go through some things with him. I've decided against flying after all, the times of departure don't suit me. I thought we'd drive instead. Would that be all right with you?"

"Yes, Matthew, but it is a long way." She was thinking it could entail an overnight stop.

He smiled, reading her thoughts. "I love driving; this restricted house-to-house process has been stifling me, I've been yearning to put my foot down on the accelerator for a long time. Besides, I believe you could take over now and then." He made a question of it, and she nodded. It would be easier, too, she thought, just to step into a car.

"It will be cosier coming home," he went on almost boy-ishly, "that is if Cassie – if she'll –"

"She will, and I'll fly back. No, Matthew, two's company."

"It could be for you as well. Peter might come."

"That," smiled Verity, "is finished."

The telephone rang and she picked it up. It was Bart.

"Still there?" he asked.

"Yes, Mr. Prince."

"Still coping?"

"Yes, Mr. Prince."

"Anything to tell me?"

"No – no, nothing out of the usual."

"It's a holiday week-end. I suppose you knew that?"

"I didn't, but I do know now."

A hesitancy at the other end, which, if it had not been Bart Prince, Verity would have put down to a wish to prolong the conversation.

"Well, if there's nothing –" Bart said.

"Nothing."

"Then goodnight, Miss Tyler."

"Goodnight, Mr. Prince." The receiver went down.

"Goodnight from me, too, V . . . and V, thank you, my dear." Matthew kissed her lightly and left.

Verity went soon after, went home to the worry of Robin again. She had thought that the prospect of telling Matthew about it in the near future, of asking his advice, might have helped her, but she found it hadn't. She sat at the window again, trying to find a way out, finding nothing but the same despair. She knew she could go to Adele, state the case, tell her it was up to her now to raise enough out of the jewellery that Robin had bought her to see Robin through. But Adele was not that kind, Adele would not part with any possession . . .

except Robin. So the worry still had to belong solely to Verity.

The several days left to the long week-end went too quickly for Verity. If she had been honest with herself, she would have admitted that she would have liked to have slowed up the hours, delayed the minutes. For though she was looking forward to talking to Matthew, and in those long hours on the road there would be plenty of opportunity, she found herself thinking instead of Bart ... seeing Bart's hard face, for hard and bitter it would be if he ever knew.

On the morning of the day prior to the brief vacation, she put a few things in an overnight bag. Though they would be travelling all night, and she intended, after she saw Cassandra and Matthew settled together ... or so she prayed ... to fly back at once, sometimes there could be delays.

Where the other days had flown, today seemed to drag. Now that it had come to the end, Verity wanted to get it over.

She was not busy ... invariably the day before a holiday, she remembered from Chelsea, is like that ... but at the last moment there was a customer who took her time.

Always patient, tonight Verity felt impatient. She could see a car drawn up at the kerb, and knew that Matthew was waiting.

But at last the woman went, and calling out to the car, "Don't come in, I won't be long," Verity pulled off her overall, took up her overnight bag, snapped off the lights, closed up, then ran out.

The car door was open for her, she got promptly in, and at once they started off. "You are in a hurry, Matthew!" she laughed.

"Why not?" came the answer ... only not in Matthew's voice.

Calmly, but not reducing his speed, Bart took the first corner, then with an open stretch in front of him, and no traffic to

107

impede him, he put his foot down.

Bart . . . not Matthew.

"Surprise, surprise," he said laconically as they caught the first green light and did not need to stop or reduce their speed.

"Yes," agreed Verity with a composure that she secretly marvelled at, though possibly she was beyond emotion, probably she was numbed. "I didn't expect you."

"That," he said, "must be the understatement of the year."

They both were silent after that, they had encountered an outer city traffic snarl, and it was no time, Verity accepted, to start a heated discussion. A thought struck her when, for the third time, the car was obliged to stop. She made no movement, unless her glance had gone to the door, but at once he said, "Oh, no, you don't, but just to make certain . . ." He leaned over and locked the door.

This was going too far, but Verity decided to restrain herself until they reached the suburbs with their greater possibilities. For after the suburbs they would be in the rural regions, long stretches of empty road only punctuated by towns much too far, as far as Verity was concerned, from the refuge of the city.

"Where are you going?" she asked at length.

"Where were you?"

"That was not my question."

"It was mine."

"Melbourne," she said uncaringly . . . what was there left to care about now? She knew it must sound ridiculous . . . she knew it must seem the end of the world at this moment. Much too far for a contemplated non-stop journey. She heard his low laugh, and was aware that he was thinking so, too. She knew he disbelieved her.

"We were driving right through," she defended herself. "I was going to relieve Matthew."

"Not very cosy," he commented slyly, and she rankled.

"Well, that was our plan." She barely contained herself.

"And the ultimate goal?"

"You know already."

As he still waited, she said, "I told you – Melbourne."

"I asked the *ultimate goal*. Matthew, who recently proved himself to be a very clever fellow when it comes to degrees, also proved himself years ago to be a very simple one. In short, as a boy he would always blab his intentions. He did again this time, but only the fact that you and he were using the long week-end to hit south. Not the ultimate goal." Again he waited.

"The goal," Verity said stiffly, "was Cassandra. I've seen something of Matthew this week, and I've convinced him that he's been going the wrong way with her."

"They must have been very interesting lessons." A pause as a light came up. "Practical, of course."

"Mr. Prince, what is this?" she demanded.

"Not what it looks. It looks like a kidnap, doesn't it? But it's not."

"I want to get out!" she snapped.

"You would have a long hike, we're halfway between . . ." He was silent while he estimated, then he told her. The towns made no sense to Verity, so far her Australian geography only embraced the eastern capitals.

"You're no wiser," he nodded, "then accept the fact that you'd find yourself bushed. You could hitch a lift perhaps, but out here that could be risky. A much more prudent move would be to stay where you are."

"With you?"

"Is it that awful? After all, you were going with Matthew."

"I wasn't. I mean –" She lapsed into silence. What could she say to this man?

"Not to worry," he tossed carelessly. "I believe you . . . or should I say I don't believe Matthew would ever think of anyone but Cassie." A pause that was more a probe, but Verity did not speak.

"But of all the fool schemes," Bart went on presently, "to take you along with him to state his case. No woman would ever respond to that. As a woman yourself you must have known it. But perhaps" . . . thinly . . . "you weren't thinking of Matthew and Cassandra but –"

"Or Peter," she came in quickly. "Also, you have the wrong idea. I was going with Matthew just to –" Her voice trailed off. It did seem ridiculous now.

She wondered what he would say if she added her other reason, that reason of talking with Matthew about Robin. For she could never talk to the man beside her, the man whom Adele, Robin's wife, had known . . . to use her words . . . *"very well."*

"All right," Bart was saying, "the subject is closed. Matthew is on his way to Melbourne . . . unaccompanied. I can't say how it will be on his way back, but I can hope. I suppose I should thank you, Miss Tyler, for giving my brother the general idea, though I cannot commend the manner in which you meant him to carry it out."

"It was not my thought."

"I well believe that, it's typical of the silly thing Matthew would do. All those years in university make a man so unworldly it's a laughing matter to someone on the outside." For all his scorn there was a note of envy in Bart's voice. It was not there, however, when he spoke again. "We've dealt with Matthew, with Peter. Only one Prince left. Aren't there any questions, Miss Tyler?"

"Yes. Where are you going?"

"Where are *we* going," he corrected.

"Where are we going?" she conceded thinly.

"To the first restaurant that's open so I can eat. I don't know what Matthew's arrangements were, but picking you up tonight made me miss my dinner." He half-glanced at her. "You would have been pushed, too. Have you dined?"

"I'm not hungry."

"All the same I want you to eat first."

"First?"

"Before I say what I have to say."

Angrily she asked him, "Hasn't it all been said?"

"No. As far as I'm concerned nothing has been said, I mean nothing of real importance. For marriage is important, isn't it?"

"Matthew's?"

"I said that Matthew had been dealt with. Ah, lights at last." He swept the car from the road round a semi-circular drive leading to a small diner. As he pulled up he said quite unemotionally, "No, *your* marriage, Miss Tyler."

Then: "With me."

CHAPTER VIII

IT WAS an hour afterwards, and coffee had been brought. Bart Prince had eaten a good meal, and during it he had spoken of everything, it seemed, but the subject he had exploded, for an explosion it had been, as he had stopped the car. Her marriage. To him.

Several times during the meal she had tried to break through, but he had stopped her.

"First things first."

"My marriage would be my first thing."

"Good. I'm glad to hear that. I trust, too, it will be a lasting thing."

"Mr. Prince, this is a very poor joke," she snapped.

"It is not a joke, Miss Tyler; believe me, I've never been more serious in my life."

"I would never marry you!" Verity declared.

"But you would have married Matthew . . . Peter?"

"No. I mean . . . Oh, I don't know."

"Then know this." He had leaned across the table. "You will be marrying me," he said.

"What makes you think that?" She tried to be coolly, contemptuously amused, but she knew she sounded heated and agitated.

"I know. Or at least I'm so sure of it you could call it knowledge. All the odds are stacked on my side."

"If you mean I'm with you in a place that I don't know at an hour that is getting rather late, that went out years ago. Oh,

112

I know you're a believer in propriety ... behind closed doors, I think it was you once said ... but these days I hardly think –" She stopped. He was laughing at her.

He finished his laugh, then he shook his head. "No, I was not meaning that at all. Brandy?"

As she declined, he suggested, "It might help you. I have some things to say."

She decided to accept the drink after all, and when he had poured it, she drank it so quickly that she had to follow it up at once by the coffee. She still felt the brandy burning in her ... but it lent her no courage. To make it worse he kept gazing steadily at her, and with that cool amusement that she had been unable to summon up for herself.

"Ready?" he asked presently.

"Yes."

"Then this is it. You will marry me because there is nothing else. No" ... as she went to object ... "note that I said 'nothing', not 'no one'. I know you would never lack a number of candidates. But money ... ah, that's a different thing."

"Money?" she queried.

"Which you must have. And in a sufficient degree."

"I have it now."

"For yourself ... But for your brother?"

Verity put down the coffee spoon she had taken up and nervously played with. "I believe I begin to understand," she said. "My brother's wife Adele has asked and received money from you. No doubt in the transaction, if transaction it's called, she's told you that Robin's remittances have not been so satisfactory of late."

"Yes," he nodded coolly, "I did give Dellie a cheque."

"For old times' sake." Verity's voice was pinched.

He was looking at her closely. He seemed amused again. "Jealous?" he asked.

"Jealous? Of you?"

"Why not? But then I forgot. I forgot you've only known me After. Adele knew me Before."

"Yes, she knew you very well."

"Perhaps." He shrugged. He was silent a moment. "But it was not Dellie who told me. Perhaps she gave the indication when she asked for a tide-over, but I never thought then that it could come to this."

"To what?"

"Our marriage."

"How could it come to it?"

He looked at her deliberately. Then he spoke deliberately. "By your inability, at least your solicitor's inability, to squeeze one cent from the Ramsay estate."

"But how can you know that?" she gasped. "Adele wouldn't know it."

"No, all she knows is that she'd like more money. But the male mind delves deeper. It wants to know *why* there is not the same money."

"When it doesn't concern him?"

"It concerned me."

"But – but why?"

"We will come to that later. I was up to the male mind. Remember?"

"Yes," she said in a low voice.

"After the thing that happened to me," he said a little roughly, "and I got out of Med school, I tried my hand in several avenues – advertising, law. I quite liked law, only I still had that feeling for –" He paused; it was evidently, from his expression, a bitter pause.

"However," he went on, "if it was not to be that, then I decided it didn't matter what. My mother needed me, so the other avenues went by. I wept no tears over them." He gave a short laugh.

"But I got sufficiently through law before I tossed it to enable me to get what I wanted from my brother professionals, even though I myself was only a near-professional, in other words had I been a rank outsider I might still be outside my present knowledge. The knowledge that not only is Robin Ramsay dead broke, he's in debt as well."

"Mr. Carstairs told you that?"

"No." A smile. "But I wouldn't say that I didn't get it out of him."

"I didn't think Mr. Carstairs –"

"To be fair to him I must admit I used certain methods. Like claiming you for a fiancée, for instance."

". . . You didn't !"

"He was quite delighted," reported Bart Prince, "seemed to think it was time you had a restraining hand."

"You lied to him," she exclaimed.

"Call it white-lied. The ultimate purpose deserved that adjective, anyway."

"I still don't think Mr. Carstairs should have –"

"Look, you have more serious things to consider just now than your solicitor's scruples. You have your brother. Where are you finding next week's cheque?"

"I can't. But" . . . proudly . . . "that doesn't mean that I'd –"

"Marry to assure it? I'm not so sure about that. You think the world of him, don't you?"

"Yes. But if I told him, Robin would understand."

"But would you tell him?"

"Yes. I mean –" Suddenly unable to cope, Verity put her face in her hands.

She was aware of his getting her to her feet, leading her out

115

of the restaurant, sheltering her all the way from curious eyes, to the car. His grasp was gentle, considerate, and the gentle consideration, so unexpected, was her undoing. The moment she gained the seclusion and privacy of the parked vehicle, she burst into tears.

"Robin is dying," she said desperately.

"I know, Verity." He said her name again, something he had not said for some time.

"If I tell him, then Adele will find out, possibly leave him."

"Yes, quite possibly."

"*You* can say that?" For a moment the grief left her; it seemed an odd agreement from a man who had known a woman "very well."

"Skip it," he said of her surprise. "Get on to facts. Adele would leave him, as you said, and would it matter?"

"Very much. Whether it's his present condition or whether this time he really cares, I don't know, all I do know is that for the little time left —"

"He must not know, he must live as he always has lived?"

"Yes."

"Then," he said deliberately, "you have no other choice than marriage with me. Oh" . . . as she went to object . . . "you could have, I suppose. You're certainly attractive enough to marry well. But rich men don't grow on trees, and even if they did, the actual clinching takes time, doesn't it? And time is something you don't have, Verity, but" . . . a significant pause . . . "you have me.

"I'm rich, and though compared to my brothers I'm no catch physically, I've still seen to it that I'm not . . . physically speaking again . . . a total loss."

. . . No, not with that deliberate whipcord strength, she thought.

"In other words, I'm bad, but I could be worse. Ordinarily

116

you'd be a fool even to consider me, but it's *extra*ordinary now, isn't it? Also there's that old enemy time."

"Mr. Prince" . . . she could not say Bart . . . "I can't believe all this."

"Then believe it," he advised her.

"But – but even if I do, what do you – what do you –" Her voice stammered to a silence.

"What do I get out of it? I think that's what you're trying to say."

"Yes."

"I can only tell you part, and this is the part: I get a satisfaction. A satisfaction that I'm acquiring something that my two brothers undoubtedly thought about . . . oh, yes, I know Peter, and even though I said what I did of Matthew and Cassandra, I know that Matthew is not that unworldly that he doesn't recognize beauty other than Cassie's. A satisfaction that an ugly wreck like I am can still show them something. A satisfaction –"

"Stop!" Verity interrupted at last.

But when he did all she could say was, "I'm not beautiful." She could not find the words for the disgust she felt.

"I think you are," he stated. But there was no feeling at all when he said it. "I think you're very beautiful, and I consider I would be very well recompensed."

"Recompensed?"

"By what you would give me in return. I would be the cripple with the lovely wife. And for that little thing, that triumph, your brother need never know the truth."

"It's horrible! I'm not listening."

"It's not a charming story, I'll give in, but you are listening, and you'll agree."

"What about – Priscilla?" she barely whispered.

"Well what about her?" he asked back.

Verity looked at him incredulously. Did anything matter to this man, anything at all? Because he would score more of a triumph by marrying someone his brother might have thought of . . . his own words . . . he would pass over Priscilla as though she never existed. And Cilla, she thought, quiet, unassuming Cilla, would never utter a word.

"It's impossible!" she said sharply.

"You're not answering yet, you're sleeping on it. Oh, no, my dear" . . . at her quick look . . . "in your own bed. As so you so triumphantly told me *that* doesn't matter any more. For which reason I'm taking you home now to do some serious thinking. Think all tonight . . . tomorrow . . . the next day. You have the entire week-end. It's happened quite opportunely, actually." He started the engine, and the car completed the half-circle of the drive.

They spoke little on the return trip. Once he glanced at his watch and remarked on the wonder of flying, how already Matthew and Cassandra would be reunited, how –

Verity turned away.

But she could not keep turning away. That fact came home to her, as, having left her at the flat, she ran upstairs and opened up to find a note pushed under the door. It was in Adele's writing, and for Adele to have called personally Verity knew the matter would be urgent. She tore away the envelope.

Adele had gone straight to the point. She had written:

"What's happened to our money? Robin had a bad attack today and our doctor called in some specialists in Robin's trouble. These men are coming again tomorrow, and, as you can guess, these private calls cost the world. There is also special medicine, and a nurse will be required. For heaven's sake, Verity, do something."

Verity read it again. Then she put the letter down. She had never felt so heavy, so burdened in all her life.

118

There seemed no way out. Except . . .

There was no awakening in the morning, for though at last she had left her seat by the window and gone to bed, she had not slept.

She wished the week-end was an ordinary working one, for then she could have occupied herself in the Castle, escaped, even briefly, from her crowding thoughts. But also she would have had the likelihood of Bart calling in upon her, waiting for her decision, even though he had assured her that she was not to answer him yet.

She did not know which would have been the most racking: the unnerving possibility of Bart – or her aching thoughts of Robin. For those thoughts . . . those memories . . . kept flashing through her tortured mind like the facets in a kaleidoscope. Robin, as the baby brother she had carried everywhere, Robin, as the toddler to whom she had taught his first steps, Robin, the schoolboy, getting help with his homework, Robin, the adolescent, getting help with his pocket money, Robin, the man, getting help with his love affairs. Robin . . . since he was Robin.

She supposed she had adored him so much because there had been no one else. There had been the warmest of feelings between her mother and herself, but her mother's real love had gone to the kindly man who had come later into her life to make a rich happiness out of her poor remnants. Louis had been sweet, and Verity had been glad Mother had returned his feelings for her. Most of all she had been glad that between them they had made Robin for her. "He's your baby," they had said.

And now the baby was a man, and the man was dying. Robin was dying. She felt she could not bear it, her grief seemed large enough to fill an eternity. But whatever she felt, the sit-

uation still existed. All she could do was keep it from Robin
. . . from Adele. Just as she had spared the little boy, she must
spare the man. And she was going to spare him.

So on the evening before her return to work, she picked up
the phone and dialled Bart's own number.

His voice came back immediately, he must have been waiting there. "Verity?"

"How did – how did you know?"

"I think I know everything about you. You haven't slept,
you haven't eaten, you've gone through every possible means
of escape." A dry laugh at that choice of words. "You've
turned over pictures in your mind of what-once-was until the
torture was unbearable. And now you're ringing to tell me –"

"Go on, please, Bart."

"No, *you* must say it." There was a final note in his voice
and she knew there would be no compromise.

"Then – it's yes," she said.

Now there was a silence at the other end, and for a hideous
moment she wondered if he had been joking with her, if it had
all been a kind of game. If he had, she thought . . .

"Thank you." His voice came at last. It came as though he
was speaking from a long way off.

"Will you call at the Castle tomorrow to tell me?" She was
actually trembling and she hoped he didn't hear it in her
voice. "I mean – tell me – when? – That is – I mean –"

"No," he said, and the tone came stronger this time. "No,
we'll be married by then."

"We couldn't!" she gasped.

"But we shall. You can do your shopping in the morning
while I see to the necessary details. Then in the afternoon –"

She was holding on to the receiver so tightly that her fingers
hurt. She couldn't go into it that fast, she was thinking, she
had to have more time.

As if he read her over the wires as well as face-to-face, he drawled, "On second thoughts we'll start life as we intend to go on, doing all things together. You can come with me while we fill in the necessary papers – probably you'll be needed there, anyway – and I'll help you shop."

"I don't need anything." She said it blankly, just for something to say while she still withdrew from what he had just told her, and she was unprepared for his quick reply.

"Certainly you'll need things. How often do you think I've been married? At least my bride will wear a new gown."

"But I have dresses."

"*The* dress?"

"Well, I –"

"Or something suitable in navy?"

"It is, as it happens."

"It won't happen."

"Then – what about –?"

"I'll tell you when I see it."

She was quiet a moment. Then: "What about the Castle?" she asked.

"As we've concluded our assessing, Cilla can open up, keep an eye on the sales . . . for that matter she can close the shop section altogether, just attend to the accounts."

"Poor Cilla!" It was out before she knew it. Now the man must say something, she thought.

"Yes, poor Cilla," he agreed. Then, at once: "Tomorrow at nine, Verity."

She held on to the phone for minutes after he had rung off.

During the evening the phone pealed again. She looked at it warily. What did Bart Prince want now?

It was not Bart, it was Adele.

"The specialists have just left. Robin seems to be reacting favourably . . . well, anyway, he does seem as good as can be

121

expected, to use the old hospital phrase."

"That's grand news."

"So was the cheque. You've certainly achieved something at last."

"You – you got it?"

"Yes. – Well, I thought I'd let you know about Rob."

Again the other end of the phone went down before Verity could cradle her own end.

Bart, she was thinking, had wasted no time. That was good for Robbie, so therefore it must be good, too, for her. Only Robin mattered, and she was grateful that Bart had acted at once. But the signed, sealed and delivered feeling that was encompassing her frightened her. It's too late, she thought, to go back now. Perhaps I could cheat, now that Adele has received the money, but other cheques will be needed. I'm closed in. I can't get out. Bart said nothing in navy blue, but I feel it should be black . . .

It was gold. Not the warm gold of the sun but the faintly green-gold of a young acorn. From the dress department they went to the jewellery for a circle of yellow sapphires for Verity's engagement ring, a plain band to be tried for size for her wedding ring. For a string of amber to lighten up the dress.

"Now you're an acorn," Bart said.

"Usually it's a flower," she said for something to say.

"Flowers fade. You can keep an acorn in your pocket for years."

"I know," she nodded, still using words to hide behind. "You don't get rheumatism and you won't grow old."

He shrugged. "I only know the years," he told her. "If I leave you now will you promise not to disappear by two o' clock?"

"Is that – when –?" She had been beside him when the ar-

122

rangements had been made, but she realized now she barely had heard a word.

"Near enough," he said. "Will you promise?"

"But I couldn't not promise, could I? I mean it's too late. You see Adele rang and –" She stopped at a look on his face.

It was there so briefly she could not have said that it was what she first had felt ... pain. At once the look was impersonal again, nothing at all conveyed.

"Yes, a little late," he agreed coolly. "Two, then?"

"Two." She got off at the beauty shop and went through the usual ritual. – Afterwards Adele told her that she had rung and rung ... rung the Castle ... rung the flat. Rung to tell her that –

At two Bart came to the beauticians and took her to a small hotel where everything was laid out in readiness – dress, shoes, all she needed. She did not ask who had done it, there could be no one else but Bart.

She dressed, went downstairs, they drove round to the church that Bart had arranged, and were married within the hour.

An hour *after* Robin had died.

Only a witness supplied by the minister stood at the ceremony, and there was no one but themselves at the dinner in the same little hotel where Verity had changed.

They sat at the candled table opposite to each other, and Bart, lifting his wine glass, said: "There, it wasn't so bad, was it?"

"No," she answered him indistinctly, for she was all choked up.

She seemed to be thinking in too many channels at the same time, yet she still did not want to direct her tumbled thoughts into one channel, because she knew now what that

123

channel would be. For ever since the simple service her awareness had kept returning to that *incredulous but unmistakable serenity that she had experienced as she had stood beside Bart Prince and made her vows.* It had been so totally unexpected she still could not believe it, and yet it had existed, it had been there, a peace of mind she had never known before. And a happiness. – Happiness?

But she could never tell him. Not this man who had gone into marriage with her for as well as an undisclosed reason ... what reason? she wondered briefly ... for the blatantly admitted reason of establishing himself in the eyes of the outsider. To use Bart's own unadorned words: "To get something that my two brothers undoubtedly thought about. – A satisfaction than an ugly wreck can still show them something."

No, she could never tell him how she felt after that.

"When we're done," Bart said, "we're going up to the Mountains." At a look on Verity's face, as, as always, she thought of Robin, he reassured her: "I'll leave Cilla a number." He paused a little diffidently. "It won't be much of a break, Verity, but we can catch up later."

She said something trite about the mountains being new to her, anyway, avoiding his eyes as she said it, suddenly almost girlishly shy because of those unfolding minutes standing beside him and knowing something so intrinsic she was afraid now to try to recapture it. And so they finished the dinner.

She went upstairs and packed her few things, very conscious of Bart standing behind her in the room ... and why not, it was their room? ... as he said: "It's only the night, Verity, so just take a few articles. One day" ... a pause ... "we'll do it all properly."

She did not know quite what he meant by that until two hours later when they had reached the mountain town with the Swiss-inspired hotel where they were to lodge.

The air smelled of wet violets and fir trees, and there was a fire crackling in the suite to which they had been led ... a large bedroom, a smaller annexe with a bed, bathroom and dining alcove.

"It's an apartment," Verity cried.

He was putting her bag on the big bed, and he did not look at her as he said: "Yes." Then he paused. "You see, Verity, tonight this room is yours."

"What, Bart?" She looked round at him, but his glance was still averted.

Then he turned suddenly, and held her eyes until she lowered her gaze.

"We've a long way to go and all our lives to complete the journey. You're tired ... you're strung-up. So, little one, good night." He stepped towards her and lightly kissed her brow. It was the first time he had kissed her since the minister had smiled at them in the church and intoned: "The groom will now kiss the bride."

"But Bart –" She spoke impulsively, and he turned instantly, a world of eager inquiry, had Verity looked up into his dark eyes. But Verity's glance stayed down.

"Yes?" he asked.

"Bart, I'm not a child ... far from it. I mean I've mothered Robin all these years. What I really mean is – I'm adult. I understand that a man and a woman –"

"I'm glad you understand that." There was no eagerness in him now, rather a cool acceptance of basic facts. "Because I do intend us to live a full life."

"You may reassure yourself." In her shyness, she said it a little stiffly, she still did not look up, and when he did not respond, she burst out: "I'll keep my side of the bargain, never fear."

"Bargain!" He said it so faintly she was not sure she really heard it. When she did bring herself to turn round, he had left the room.

She could hear him in the annexe next door, moving around, probably taking out his things. Then she heard the door close between them . . . then his light snap out.

She put her own light out and undressed in the dark. Then, tremblingly, she got into bed. She felt sure she would not sleep, but when the telephone rang some hours later she woke up with a start.

Before she could grope for the receiver, Bart was there, already in his dressing gown although it had barely begun to peal. He took it up and asked: "Yes?" Then he said: "Yes. — Yes, I do understand. — Yes, I'll do that. — Yes." He put the phone down.

Already she was going off to sleep again, and for a long moment he stood looking down on her, she could see him faintly through her almost closed eyes, and for a second —

"Yes, Bart?"

"It's nothing. Go to sleep." He went out.

She did sleep. She slept until the next morning, and Bart standing beside her with coffee. He was dressed ready to leave. He had been right when he had said it would only be a brief break.

"Drink it, Verity." Something in his voice made her look quickly up at him.

"What is it?" she asked.

"Coffee."

"I didn't mean that, I meant —"

"Drink it first." He said it authoritatively, and after a moment she did so. He waited until she drained the final drop, then he said quietly: "That ring last night."

"Oh, yes?" Only now did she remember it.

126

"It was a message for you."

"For me?" She sat up straighter.

"From Cilla."

"Oh." She relaxed back again.

"You see" . . . gently . . . "Adele had been trying to get you, and when she failed she finally got Priscilla's home."

"Adele trying to get me? Bart – Bart – not Robin?"

"Yes, little one." He sat down on the bed beside her.

"He's – worse?"

"No, Verity. No. It's all over."

"All over?" She looked at him stupidly. For a moment she thought: Robin's better. The nightmare is finished. Robin is all right again.

And then the meaning of Bart's words became clear.

"No!" she cried.

"I'm sorry, but yes, Verity."

"And that was the phone call last night?"

"Yes."

"You should have told me."

"There was nothing to be done. I wanted you to have a night's rest at least. Besides, it had already been over for some hours."

For a while what he said did not sink in. Then Verity said in a muffled voice: "How many hours?"

"Does it matter?" he answered harshly, and but for the harshness she would have left it at that.

"Yes," she said, her pain because of Robin making her unreasonable, for what she said then she did not really mean. "Yes. Because I think you knew before you married me. Because if I'd known, I needn't have gone through this thing. I mean –"

She stopped at his hand on her, hard, relentless.

"I didn't know, but had I known I would have done just what you said."

"To even up with your brothers." She shivered. "To show them something?"

"Verity . . ." he began.

"Isn't it true? Didn't you give me that reason? That reason for this – this farce?" She was looking down at her ring.

"Verity . . ."

"To establish yourself, you said. To show them. And because of Robbie, I agreed. And now Robbie has died too early." She stopped to put a shaking hand to her quivering mouth. "And I've found out – too late."

CHAPTER IX

THEY drove down to Sydney with the separation between two seats . . . and a world . . . dividing them. Neither of them spoke for the two hours that it took.

Only when they joined the snarl of the city traffic did Bart address Verity.

"I'll take you straight to your brother's apartment. Have you any money for the taxi fare home?"

Home? But where was home? When two people married it was presumed that they lived together. But she – But Bart –

Reading her thoughts, he said sharply, "Our home, of course." For a moment he took his eyes away from the stream of cars to give her a quick searching look.

"I may be late." She did not look back at him. "I'll have to go to my own flat to pick up some things."

"That can be attended to tomorrow."

She said stiffly, "Very well . . . but I still can't say what time it will be."

"That's all right, I'll be waiting. I'll be as near as the phone."

"Thank you . . . but I don't think Adele will be requiring anything." Her voice was brittle.

His mouth tightened. "I didn't say Adele."

"No, you didn't. I'm sorry. – Yet it does come down to the same thing, doesn't it? It was only because of Adele that we –"

His face had paled with suppressed anger. "You're under

129

strain. I'm not arguing with you. Later –" He hunched one shoulder, the shoulder near hers. Briefly the pair of them touched, and she withdrew slightly. She knew he felt her withdrawal, for his tightened mouth grew even tighter. In spite of herself Verity shivered.

A few minutes afterwards he turned into a quiet avenue, went a short distance, then pulled up at the lavish block of flats where Robin and Adele . . . where *Adele* . . . lived.

"Want me to come in with you?" he asked offhandedly, and Verity knew that if he had not asked like that, she would have answered an eager Yes.

"Yes," she would have appealed, "yes, Bart." For, looking up at the window at which Robbie often had sat, she longed for someone's hand now in hers. – But it could not be Bart's hand. Not with a carelessly tossed offer like that.

"No, thank you." She got out of the car.

"I'll be waiting," he said again.

"It will be late." It was her turn to repeat herself.

"It doesn't matter what time it is." He did not move the car until she entered the building.

When she heard him leave . . . she did not look around to see . . . she knew a sudden devastating emptiness. She had never enjoyed coming to this apartment, Adele had not welcomed her, Robin had looked more ill each time she saw him. And now . . . and now . . .

She went into the lift and pressed the button to Robin's . . . *Adele*'s floor.

Adele opened the door to her. She looked pale and shocked; at least Verity had to credit her with that. She led the way into the lounge.

"I knew it was going to come," the girl said as she lit a cigarette, "but I didn't expect it this soon. Also, when it happens, you're still not prepared, are you?"

130

"Was he in pain?" Robin always had been a bad sufferer, Verity thought tenderly; as a little boy he had cried over a cut knee, created over a stubbed toe. There had to be heaps of love administered as well as salve and bandages.

"No, he was sedated. Poor Rob!" Adele exhaled.

"I suppose," she said presently, "I come out of this as the archdemoness of all times, or whatever a female demon is. I know I'm an unrewarding character ... your word, Verity ... but I haven't had the most rewarding of experiences." – She had said this before, recalled Verity.

For a few moments the girl brooded, presumably over her unrewarded past, and, suddenly, unbidden, Bart came flashing into Verity's mind, Bart who had known "Dellie" *very well*. Yet still never married her. Had that been the less-than-reward she spoke of now?

"But with favourable circumstances I would have stuck with Rob," went on Adele. "He was the same type as I am, really. You mightn't like that, but we suited. Anyway" ... a shrug ... "it's all over now." She looked at Verity. "Anything you want? Sentimental section, naturally, working with the Princes you would never lack anything monetarily." She gave a short laugh.

Working with the Princes ... So Adele did not know about them. Priscilla did not know either. No one knew. We could be – not married, Verity thought.

"I want nothing, thank you, Adele." All she needed of Robin, Verity knew, was imprinted on her heart.

She wondered when she should break it to Adele that Robbie had not died the rich man his wife had thought. Not yet ... though already Adele looked much more composed than she had been when she had opened the door.

"When is the –" Verity began quietly.

Adele understood. "Tomorrow. Early." She gave a little shiver. "I hate these things."

Impulsively Verity said: "Would you like me to stop tonight?"

"Would you?" rushed Adele. "Bart brought you, didn't he? I saw his car pull up. I'll ring and tell him what's what. No" ... as Verity moved forward ... "I know the number I should." She crossed to the phone.

I know the number. I should. As she listened to Adele dialling Bart's apartment, Verity could not help herself wondering how many times Adele had done this before. Bart had never denied he had known Adele "very well". What had been between them?

She moved sensitively away again ... but she could not move away from her own nagging thoughts.

Had Adele's failure to tie Bart up been the incentive for Adele to marry Robin so promptly, for it had been all over by the time she had arrived from England. This was the painful trend of the thoughts.

Then ... following fast, following compulsively: Had that marriage been the "other" reason to Bart's frankly admitted one of "status", the one that had *really* urged him to force along his own marriage, to her, that reason as old as society itself; that retaliatory what you did, I can do, too, Adele.

He could have called on Priscilla, Verity thought abstractedly, sweet, loving Cilla, but his Cilla would be such an accustomed figure she would probably never occur to him for that. Possibly only his mother ... and Priscilla herself ... had dreamed in such a strain. But Verity Tyler was unaccustomed, so she did occur. She was also immediately available, because she was at her wits' end. Bart had known it. He had known he could make that tit-for-tat move at once. So he had married her. She was Mrs. Bartley Prince. She was Bart's wife for two

reasons. Achievement. Repayment. But not for ... never for
...

She felt a throbbing in her head as she tried to work it all
out, but in spite of her vagueness, and the distance she had put
between herself and the phone, she still heard Adele.

"It's Dellie, Bart ... Thank you, my dear ... No, so far
I'm holding up well. Verity will stay with me tonight, you
know me of old, how I go to pieces. Yes ... Yes, Bart, I'll be
here ... I'll be waiting."

The phone went down.

Thank you, my dear ... You know me of old.

Verity was still mulling over Adele's conversation long after
she had put Adele to bed, then gone herself. She had finished
her tears for Robin, she had accepted with final resignation
the futility of grief. But she could not accept Adele's soft
words, she found. Even when she pulled the pillow over her
ears she still listened in retrospect. My dear. You know me of
old. There had been something else, she recalled dully. It had
been : "I'll be here." Then : "I'll be waiting."

Why had Adele said that?

The funeral service was short. Only Robin's wife and sister
attended. When it was over, Adele said, "Thank you, Verity,"
and got in her car and left at once. A little confused, for she
had believed Adele would need her longer, Verity called a
taxi and went out to Balmain.

Once there she moved around the rooms, picking up things,
putting them down again, oddly restless. She remembered to
ring the agent to cancel the flat, she remembered to stop the
milk, the bread – then that was that, she thought. Now she
could leave. Go – home, as Bart had said. But all at once she
knew she could not go without a previous word from Bart.
Kind, or otherwise, but he had to tell her first. She dialled the

number that Adele had dialled so much more expertly last night. She listened to the bell ring at Bart's end. There was no answer. She tried again, but still no answer. She put the phone down, feeling inexplicably hollow and very alone.

She knew she needed somebody, some human contact. She rang Woman's Castle, but either Priscilla had not come in, or was busy, but again there was no response.

She decided to ring Adele, ask her how she was feeling. The girl had made it obvious that she was finished with her, that she needed her no longer, but all at once all Verity cared about was to hold the phone to her ear *and hear a voice*.

It rang several times, and she had just begun to wonder whether anyone was answering telephones today, when the other end was taken up.

"Hullo." It was a male voice ... and she recognized it at once as Bart's.

"Hullo," he called impatiently again.

... "Yes," Verity was remembering from Adele last night, "I'll be here. I'll be waiting."

Bart's voice called a final Hullo, then the phone went down.

But – "I'll be here. I'll be waiting." Verity still heard those words.

An hour afterwards she was still sitting there at the phone staring blankly into space. She had not thought she was so prone to pain, that is pain apart from Robbie. She had not thought, anyway, that she could feel pain because of Bart. Bart, whom, whether she had liked him or not, she had instinctively trusted, for at no time since she had entered the Prince world had she not trusted and believed Bart Prince, but now –

Clumsily, probably ineptly, since her hurt made her inept, she pieced her story together.

Adele and Bart had been close friends ... hadn't they

known each other "very well"? . . . but Adele like all women had presumably wanted marriage. Reward, she had expressed it. Bart, like all men, had wanted freedom; either that or his accident had left him with an uncertainty that had delayed any matrimonial move.

So Adele, probably in frustration, for there had certainly not been love, had married Robin, and that had prompted Bart to retaliate later in the same way. With her. He had explained it as a status gesture, and she had believed that that embittered man could be capable of such an action. She had not cared for the idea . . . what woman would care to be only an achievement symbol? . . . but now she knew she liked her present position much less. For as well as being a feather in Bart's cap as he would have her believe, she was a substitute for the girl he really had wanted, but not got around to. Not until it was too late. If he had waited another day, waited another hour, he could have rectified that hideous mistake. – And I, Verity knew hollowly, would not have made mine.

This comedy of errors that was no comedy at all she knew she could have put aside, or at least passed over, *but never, never, could she forgive Bart seeking out Adele so soon . . . going to her at once.*

What was he saying to her now in her apartment? Were there recriminations? Regrets? Plans? Hopes? Schemes like: "Wait a while." Agreements like: "Very soon." Arrangements like: "Give it time." Anticipations like: "After that . . ."

"Oh, no!" Verity said aloud. I'm not really married to Bartley Prince, she was thinking wildly, *not really*. There's a signature on a form, but we're not man and wife. When I go round to Bart's apartment tonight . . . home, he had said, she recalled with a thin little smile . . . it will be to hear him tell me all this, tell me that as well as my misfortune, he has a misfortune on his own hands.

135

The indignity of it all gripped fiercely at her. I can't go on, she knew, not now, nor tomorrow. Not ever.

But what do women do in a situation like this? They go away, I would know that, but where can they go? What do they live on? How do they exist? I can work like anyone else works, but if I work as I'm working now, on what I've been trained for, Bart will be sure to find me, there is a closeness in businesses like his ... and we would have that reckoning. It has to come, my common sense tells me that, but not now, not yet, not – not with Bart answering this soon from Adele's phone.

She tried desperately to think, to reason ... to plan, but she found she could get no further than that ... than Bart's voice on Adele's wire.

She had been nervously pleating a sheet of old newspaper, and, looking down, she read absently ... then not so absently ... the few lines of the advertisement in the middle column that somehow had caught her attention.

"Young Australian woman for conversation in English with two boys of eleven and thirteen years. Remote country home but every amenity and consideration. Telephone ..."

The edition, she saw, was a week old. She was not Australian. But that "remote country home", remote from the turmoil in which she now found herself, the further turmoil in which she knew she would be placed, suddenly prompted her to take up the phone. She checked the given number.

She was aware she could not indefinitely run away from Bart, but just to remove herself from the scene for days, weeks ... perhaps a month ... Just to get away ...

Verity put her finger on the first digit. The advertiser would have left by now, left with the young Australian, not English, woman; no one waited for an answer to an ad a week after. She turned round the final figure and heard a bell, and for the first time today there was a prompt reply. A young boy's voice, she judged. A pleasantly foreign voice.

"Yes?" he asked.

"I'm Verity Tyler." No, she was Verity Prince, she thought dully. "I've just read an advertisement in a week-old newspaper."

"Oh, yes," said the boy. "Will you come?"

Will you come? It seemed incredible . . . it was incredible. She listened again.

"It's a long way away," the boy went on. "All the others said too far away. It's called Tetaparilly, and that means – Oh, Mother, why can't I try this time? You did no good, and she sounds nice."

"Gunnar!" A woman's voice now came across the wire. "My sons!" she apologized to Verity with a laugh.

"This one sounded in little need of English conversation," praised Verity sincerely.

"He is the better," admitted his mother. "Ulf, the younger boy, is quite bad, I fear. It would be wonderful if you could come."

"I'm English," Verity told her.

"Better still for English conversation. We have been delayed from leaving Sydney earlier because of a throat condition in Ulf, but all is well now and the doctor says we can go at once. You could come at your convenience, of course, if you will only agree. We are a Swedish family, and have settled in the north-west. My husband and I went some years ago, then, when we could bring them over, our two young sons. It is an isolated farm, so the boys must have school by correspondence. Ordinarily they would have picked up English quite easily if they had been able to mix, but with only parents to converse with –"

"You, anyway, are very fluent," said Verity.

"Yes, we both, Big Gunnar and I, can speak English. But I assist my husband a great deal on the farm, we are little more than beginners so can afford only a minimum of help, thus I have not the time for encouraging my sons as I would like. But our place is comfortable, as the advertisement says, yet"... ruefully... "also, I must admit, remote."

"The important thing to me," Verity broke in, "is – is it still available?"

"Is it – Why, yes. *Why, yes!*" There were delighted noises at the other end. "Does this mean –"

"I want to come," Verity said.

"Then – how soon? We could forward you the plane ticket to the nearest field, and we would pick you up."

"When are you leaving?"

"As early as an hour from now," said the voice. "I am driving the car, and my husband, who has been concluding a deal at Bathurst, will meet us there. But if you could tell me when –"

There was a moment's pause from Verity, during which time she could hear the Swedish woman breathing more quickly, probably fearing she had not gained her prize after all.

Then Verity said: "Could I come with you?"

"Come with us?"

"I'm sorry, perhaps your car is not big enough –"

"Our car is very big, as well as very clumsy, the boys call it the Tank. But this is wonderful."

"You may not think so," Verity laughed.

"I do think so. I think, like Gunnar did, that you sound nice. You *are* serious?"

"Very serious. When and where?"

"Within the hour that I told you." After some consideration the woman gave Verity a meeting place that even a newcomer would have no trouble in finding. Excited, she rang off.

More slowly, Verity put down her end of the phone. She knew that what she was about to do was immature, unreasonable, quite abominable . . . but also that it was essential, essential to her own peace of mind. She could not face Bart yet. In time she could, and must, face him, but she had to have this breathing space.

She had already placed her things in her bag, so she had no packing now. She knew, though, she must leave some kind of note, otherwise Bart could think all sorts of fates for her, possibly raise an alarm.

She took out pen and paper, cursing her dullness as the clock hand went half way round the face before she could find any words to write. Then they could not have been sparser, less illuminating, though illumination was the last thing she wanted, she thought.

She wrote barely: "I have gone away. V." Then left it at that.

As she ran down the stairs, she heard her telephone ring . . . but she did not turn back.

CHAPTER X

TETAPARILLY was far north-west, and, in spite of what Grete Dahlquist had said, a well-established little station. The reason that Grete was needed to help her husband so much was a new crop they had gone in for, one that reacted favourably in most instances to a woman's hands. It was herbs.

"Our parents went in for herbs in Europe," the Swedish couple explained, "and now the demand is growing out here."

They had come originally to Australia because of an inheritance. An uncle had left Gunnar the property.

"Yes, a Swede, of course," Grete had laughed. "Just look at that furniture!"

It was very old and very beautiful, Verity saw at once. The Chelsea house had handled such stuff. It was not seen much in Australia.

"No, Uncle Bent had it shipped out," Grete said when Verity remarked on this. "You find it good; we find it cumbersome. We both, my husband and I, incline to the modern pieces that our Nordic countries are now doing so beautifully. In fact we incline so much that we have already been doing some shipping out ourselves." She showed Verity the slim functional pieces that had arrived with much pride. "You do not like them?" she laughed.

"I do. Yet not so much in comparison. But perhaps I'm the old-fashioned type. What I definitely do not like is seeing them mixed up together."

"Neither do we, but slowly ... slowly ..." Grete Dahlquist spread her capable hands.

"You will sell the old stuff?"

"We have been selling ever since Big Gunnar and I started here." Grete often called her husband Big Gunnar. "As we gain a new piece, we sell Uncle Bent's old things. I'm sorry we disappoint you" ... another laugh ... "but it is balanced because you never disappoint us. We still can't believe our good fortune."

"You don't really disappoint me," refused Verity. "Your selections are in excellent taste, it's just that I like old things."

"In a new country?"

"It is old, too."

"Oh, yes, we have learned about that, also, but not old furniture old, at least not for us." Grete put her arm round Verity and they walked down to the herb section that was the Swedish woman's dream.

"I love it," she had confessed. "Do you think badly of me for preferring to raise a bed of rue to teaching my boys to enunciate more properly?"

"I think it shows your love of them to pay for me to do so."

"Not much, I'm afraid." Grete had looked worried. The salary was not large, but out here Verity did not need a large salary. She had everything she wanted. Most of all, a less troubled heart.

She liked the young couple very much, for they were still that in spite of their tall sons. "We were married early," Grete had said.

They had left the boys with her parents at the ages of seven and nine, Grete returning several times in the intervening years to see them, then at the end of that period bringing them out with her.

"They love it, as we do. They like new things, as we do.

141

Hence poor Uncle Bent's furniture." Another laugh. She was a happy person and laughed a lot.

From the moment the Tank had pulled up at the rendezvous that had been chosen, Verity had known she would be as happy as she could be anywhere with this nice family. When Big Gunnar had joined them in Bathurst and taken over the wheel, she had felt more confident still.

The homestead had proved a delight. Instead of the accepted spreading, leisurely one-storey edifice favoured in most instances, it had borrowed from native Sweden. It was a surprise to come across its three levels and its tucked-in attics and dormer windows, but it was a pleasant surprise.

The boys were likeable, and she felt they liked her. Big Gunnar had built a swimming pool, she had a mount to go riding with Gunnar and Ulf, in fact she could think of nothing that she needed.

Grete chatted about everything, but she never intruded into Verity's life. If Verity told her anything, she listened very eagerly, so Verity guessed she must be curious about her. But she never asked, and Verity never confided. Anyway, she thought, what would I have to say? You can't talk about emptiness.

There was a mixed plate at Tetaparilly, as Gunnar Dahlquist put it. A little sheep. A few cattle. A lot of crops. Their new herbs. Then they had leased the western and southern sections to a cotton starter. It was two weeks before Verity met Chris Boliver.

Grete had made only a superficial endeavour to hide her eagerness for Verity and Chris to like each other. "It is not good Chris living as he lives," she said. Then carefully, but still saying it : "It is not good for you, Verity."

"I'm contented, thank you, Grete." Verity was. – Well, she was as contented, anyway, as she could hope to be. At times the enormity of the things she had done, that outrageous walk-

142

ing out from her marriage without an explanation, with only: "I have gone away. V," did appal her, as in all fairness she knew it should, but in between she knew a degree of serenity out in this serene western refuge, with its wide unclouded skies, its distant horizons, and its nice people, for already she liked them, parents and children, very much. She was aware that Grete wanted her to like their neighbour, too.

Well, she was prepared ... a little ... for that. She was young, and at times she thought wistfully of younger company than Grete's and Big Gunnar's, yet older than the boys'. But it must stop at that. She knew it, but Grete didn't, and she listened rather uneasily as Grete explained how Chris was American, but had left his native cotton fields to start again in Australia after his young wife had died.

"I know what you will be thinking now," Grete had babbled eagerly. "You will ask yourself what does this Grete want me to do, live with a ghost? And I would say yes, for I believe from what Chris has told me it is a happy ghost, and I believe from my own knowledge that it should be so. Male and female, Verity. Why do you think I left my children all those years for my mother to bring up? I missed them terribly, but I knew, anyway, they were only on loan to me, but that my husband was for ever. Two people together is as it should be. Don't you think?"

"But, Grete, you don't understand ... and I'm afraid I can't tell you."

"Then you, too, have thoughts behind you. Then I think it could be very good for you and Chris to –"

"*Grete!*"

"I'm sorry. Big Gunnar always says I rush in. It is just that I'd like you for a neighbour one day, Verity."

"I'd like you, Grete, but –"

"Then do not say any more. Wait till you meet our Chris."

With a sigh Verity had decided to leave it at that.

Chris Boliver came riding up one morning just before Verity's hour of conversation with Gunnar and Ulf.

"Look at him," said Grete as the fair American on the grey horse approached, "he has a large car and a landrover, but he rides." An inspiration came to her. "Why don't you ride with him, Verity?"

Verity burst out laughing.

"You are supposed to be asked," she pointed out. "I could hardly go up to Mr. Boliver and say 'Come riding with me.'"

"No," agreed a soft American drawl, and Verity realized her voice had carried in the clear air, "but you could say to *Chris* Boliver, 'Come riding with me.'"

"And your answer, Chris?" Grete came in eagerly.

"Yes, please," said Chris at once, his hazel eyes appreciatively on Verity.

He said he could do with English conversation, too, after all he also was a foreigner, and he followed Gunnar and Ulf into the schoolroom. Embarrassed at first, Verity found herself enjoying the hour. They compared their brands of English, the American way, the English way, the Swedish–Australian variety, for Gunnar and Ulf talked a mixture of what they had picked up from the farm hands and their parents' native tongue.

It became an established thing in the week that followed for Chris to "happen" along. That was what he always said. "I happened along."

When she laughed at him, he asked, "What would you say?"

"I came."

"I came, I saw . . . I conquered?"

Flushing, Verity started on other varieties of differences . . . paraffin where the Australian said kerosene, supper that meant a snack before bed in Australia but in England and America meant what the Australians called tea. She was aware that Chris was looking at her and not listening as attentively as she liked Gunnar and Ulf to listen. – She was aware, too, of her awareness of him. I must stop it, she knew.

A few days afterwards he said diffidently, "Knowing Grete, I have no doubt she has spoken about me, Verity."

"Well – yes."

"I was married. When Elvie died I knew I must get away. There will never be anyone like Elvie, yet would I want that? – Yet more important, would the one I now want want that?"

"I wouldn't know, Chris," she said honestly.

"Then I'm asking you to think about it, Verity. I can't offer you what I had for Elvie, but I can offer you what Elvie never had of me. She was my morning time, something that happens only once in a man's life. But a day can grow as lovely in a different way. The thing is whichever view you take, the day *will* grow, will reach night. So all the trying in the world to hold time back still will never hold it. Life must go on. Do you follow me, Verity?

"Yes. – Grete has been talking to you."

"She has," he admitted, "but I think I would still have reached this knowledge of my own accord, this acceptance that I can't live the rest of my days on only a dream. I've a lot of days yet, you see."

"I hope so, Chris. But Chris –"

"Yes, I know. There is something, too, with you. I could tell it at once when I first met you. Perhaps you're only at the stage that I was when I came out here. Still withdrawing from it all. But it will pass, Verity. And then –"

It will pass. Verity gave a bleak little smile. Oh, Chris dear, if you only knew!

He took her silence for thoughtfulness, and touched her shoulder gently.

"Think about it, anyway, Verity."

She could not reply to that.

The Dahlquists had taken delivery of some more of their chosen furniture. Plain, unpolished, simple to sparse in line though it was, Verity had to admit that the almost Biblical quality of this remote western terrain set off the uncluttered designs in cool perfecion.

"I knew you would see it in time," Grete nodded eagerly. "To put scrolls and curlicues in this basic land would be very wrong."

"Your uncle did it."

"Big Gunnar's dear old Uncle Bent. But that was years ago. Now his nephew is selling it."

"Surely not to anywhere at all?" asked Verity, shocked.

"Oh, no, we have our own dear man, our very dear man, and he has made us promise that we sell only to him. Each time we have a few pieces to let go to make room for the new, he comes and buys it."

"That is good." Verity felt relieved. She was still sufficiently the connoisseur to shudder at any indiscriminate disposal of such lovely stuff.

It was a month now since Robin had died ... so a month since she had married Bart Prince. Common sense told her that she must make a move soon, she had had her respite, had her time for constructive thought ... even though she had done very little of that ... and she could not go on like this. She must contact Bart, tell him he could start procedures, or whatever one did to begin a release. A release so he could go to Adele.

As it always did when she thought of Bart and Adele, the picture of Priscilla came to Verity's mind. Dear background Priscilla, whom once she had coupled with Bart, when all the time it had been her brother's wife. But even Mrs. Prince had assumed it was Bart and Priscilla, Verity recalled.

Priscilla was too worthwhile not to belong to someone, Verity's thoughts ran on. Then she smiled reprovingly at herself. I'm becoming a Grete, she accused.

Yet with little else to think about out here, it was a diversion, and she even got to the extent of bringing Priscilla and Chris together in her mind. – But at that she stopped, stopped at the thought of Chris's fair good looks, his serious gold-green eyes.

I am beginning to like him, she thought, appalled, and I can't, I mustn't.

She knew she could not go on much longer like this. But before she could do anything, admit what she should have told Gunnar and Grete . . . and Chris . . . right from the beginning something else happened to put any telling back for yet another day.

And a night. . . .

As Chris smilingly put it as he extended one arm of his jacket to include Verity, in olden days . . . as younger Gunnar and Ulf always expressed anything further back than their own years . . . this episode certainly would have "fixed things."

– "Even still does in some straitlaced New England towns," he admitted.

"How do you mean fixed?" Verity had been fastening herself in from the breeze biting at the other side from Chris.

"You shock me, Verity," he had teased. "Us, of course. This is unconventional, to say the least."

"Your coat? I find it warm and necessary."

"Can you find me necessary, too?" Chris had said then.

Before their predicament he had taken her out to see, and understand, he hoped, the cotton. "Elvie understood the process perfectly." He had pulled himself up sharply. "I'm sorry,

Verity," he had apologized at once.

"For what?"

"For bringing in Elvie."

"Oh, Chris, don't feel like that, keep keeping her in your mind."

"You don't mind?"

"I want you to."

"But if we –"

"Not now, Chris," she had evaded, reading his thoughts. But it had to be some time, her own thoughts had warned. She must not keep on like this.

They had gone through the different processes of the cotton. Chris even had shown Verity where he planned a future ginnery. He had said deprecatingly, "And I can have it, Verity. I really mean I have the means . . . I think you have the right to know that. You wouldn't be . . . well, I'm not a poor man."

And you, knew Verity wretchedly, have the right to know that I have a husband with more than just means, a rich husband, only he isn't really, because we – because I –

"Verity, didn't you like me telling you that?" Chris had asked with concern at her preoccupied silence.

"Telling me what?" She realized she had not been listening with attention, she had been thinking of something else.

"Money."

"Of course I didn't mind. And Chris, I love the source of your money. I love the cotton. I love those fluffy balls."

"Bridal," he had agreed, and as it often . . . unbidden . . . seemed to happen, he seemed to withdraw from her into another world. Poor Chris!

They had had a happy meal at his house before they had set out on the ride to the distant rocks that Verity always had wanted to see.

"I'm going to give you some good American fare," Chris had

told her. "I thought it would make a change from Swedish."

."And Australian – don't forget we have Australian hands, and to them all the choice Swedish offering in the world would not come up to steak and damper. But this looks wonderful, Chris. Is it –" She had examined the perfectly baked pie.

"Blueberry. From a can. But the pastry is my own doing. If it adds a few points to my score, it will be worth my having thrown out four pies before this one."

"Did you, Chris?"

"Yes. I remember once we were having a blueberry contest, Elvie and I, and –" As before, he stopped abruptly.

"It's a beautiful pie," Verity had come in quickly. Then she had said spontaneously: "You're wonderful husband material, Chris." As abruptly as he had, she had stopped, too.

They had both looked at each other, then smiled ruefully. He is completely nice, Verity had thought with a little catch at her heart.

The Outcrop was the only higher point in a vast world of plain. Once, Verity had been told, it would have been a mountain, but centuries of centuries had worn the mountain down to the small but in this flat country salient rise that it was now.

Because of its position it seemed to entrap every colour that the day chose to wear. Crimson in the morning. Pure amber at noon. Purples and deep burgundies at night. Verity had never got over turning to gaze at it and wondering what it would be like to gaze back from.

"Probably," Grete had warned, "it will be the same as the house with the golden windows, and we will have the colours."

"It must still be fine to stand there and look around."

Chris must have heard her say that, for as soon as the meal was over after the cotton inspection, he had said they would go across.

At first he had suggested taking his Rover to the closest

149

point, then they could climb up, but Verity had wanted to ride. If she had listened to him, she told him ruefully as later he had apportioned out his jacket, they would not be up here like this.

"I'm not complaining."

"But you did say about this 'fixing' it," she reminded him with a giggle.

"Perhaps wishfully," he suggested.

They had ridden as far as they could, then left their horses cropping. That, Chris had said, was where he had to take the blame, but Nomad had never needed before to be tethered. However, something must have scared the horse, he was a highly sensitive animal, and suddenly he had galloped down the hill. Before Verity could reach her mare, Sally had followed Nomad.

The sun had been well to the western rim. Even as they had stood looking at the retreating horses, it had started to sink. Verity knew, even though she had only been here some weeks, that dusk would only be a matter of minutes. It was instant night out here in the west.

Also, although the days were warm, it would be cold with the plain all around them. She had only a thin blouse on, and she shivered at the thought of what lay ahead. – That was when Chris had apportioned out his jacket ... one arm each, which meant they had to sit very close together, as close as one, not two.

The darkest moment had been just after the sun had slipped away and after elf light had deepened into night. For this was the time of no stars, once the stars pricked out it would be almost like putting on a lamp, for out here the heavens fairly blazed.

"Verity."

She had known it was coming, but the knowledge didn't

help her now. But before Chris said anything, Verity knew what *she* had to say.

She took a deep breath.

But finally it had been hours before she could tell him. All that time he had waited sympathetically, sensing her desperate need to spill out the words, appreciating the difficulty she found in doing so. When at length she had blurted the story, he had tightened his grasp on her hand.

"I felt there was something important."

"Not really important, Chris, although we were married we're not married. I mean –"

"I know, I know." He spared her. Then, after a pause: "But does it really finish at that, Verity?"

"Chris?"

"It doesn't, does it, girl?"

"Chris, I don't understand you."

"I believe deep down you do, but you just won't let yourself believe it. But it's still there, Verity, and even if you don't, or won't, know it, then I still do. If I didn't, then . . ." He gave a little smile.

"If you didn't know what, Chris?" she asked directly.

"Your love."

"What love?"

"For this man."

"You're wrong."

"I'm not wrong, girl, and if I didn't know it, I would wait and marry you. But what would be the use of marrying half a heart."

Now she *did* understand him. She understood that he was telling her that only that he sensed the impossibility of what Grete in her goodness had tried to bring about, that he would not be saying all this now, that instead he would be –

But . . . and Verity knew it with a sudden sure perception

151

. . . Chris Boliver would *not*.

Calmly, she told him so.

He listened to her silently. He heard her say, "You still would not have married me, dear Chris, because in your heart you're still married to Elvie. Some marriages are like that." He listened to her say it in different words once again.

There was a silence. It was such a long one it seemed hours before he spoke.

Then: "Thank you, Verity," Chris said.

After a while he blurted, "I just didn't know . . . I was confused . . . I just accepted what Grete advised, and she said –"

"There should be someone again?"

"Yes."

"Yet in your heart you didn't feel it?" Now it was Verity's turn to probe.

"No."

"Then –?"

"Then it doesn't have to be." He nodded at her in the dark. "You are right. Grete was wrong. Oh, she's kind, and she means well, but . . ." Another pause. "Thank you, Verity."

After that they just sat close together, each intent on their own thoughts. At times they spoke companionably, but that was all it was. Yet Verity saw that Chris had reached a new peace of mind. Probably what Grete in her kindness had urged would do for a lot of men, most men, but not Chris. He had been uncertain, but now he had found himself. There was a tug of sadness to his mouth, that would always be there, but there was a serenity and an acceptance he had not had before.

As for herself, the relief of spilling out everything had lightened her so considerably that with the first buttering of dawn she felt almost like the new day.

Taking Chris's hand in hers, she smiled up at him, and they descended from the Outcrop to start the long trek home.

"Possibly we'll be met halfway," Chris said. "Someone will see the horses, guess what took place, and come out for us."

They had gone only a short distance when this happened. Turning a bend with a concealing mulga blotting out the track beyond it, they came almost on the car.

"Hi," called out Big Gunnar from behind the wheel, "all well and accounted for?"

"All well, all accounted for," called back Verity cheerfully, Chris's hand still in hers, her eyes still smiling because of that smile now in his. Then she froze.

Sitting beside her employer was someone she had not expected, or wanted, out here.

It was Bart.

CHAPTER XI

BART made no attempt to claim Verity, but on the other hand he prevented any move on her part to claim him by inserting blandly: "Very well, very accounted for, from the look of the victims, so your worries were unnecessary, Gunnar. Being acquainted with the lady . . . yes, I am . . . and knowing her resourcefulness" . . . the slightest of pauses . . . "I should have reassured you previously. Careless of me, my friend. I must have been concentrating on the male side of the episode. Your neighbour, Chris Boliver, I should say?"

"Yes, you can say that." Chris had stepped forward and extended a firm hand.

Verity was glad that when she had told the American her story, she had used no names. Chris had an open way with him and certainly would have registered immediate pre-knowledge of Bart. As it was, all that his likeable face expressed was a continuance of that acceptance and serenity that he had thanked Verity for up on the Outcrop.

That Bart could interpret the look as something intrinsic between the man and herself did not occur to Verity. She simply was relieved that Chris did not know, that Gunnar did not know, that Bart had the control to wait for a private moment.

Gunnar was saying, "Well, it's a small world" of Bart's casual acknowledgment of Verity. "But," he went on, "I should have known, she's so keen on furniture, and it seems you an-

154

tique people are a race apart." There was a general laugh at that "antique people" which considerably lightened the strain for Verity. She was glad when Gunnar continued, "As Grete remarked last night: 'Fancy coming out all this way for Uncle Bent's old stuff.' Yes, a race apart, as I said." Gunnar spread his hands. "Not that we would have it any other way, thank you, Bart," he hastened to add.

He turned now to his American neighbour. "Was it as we guessed, Chris? Something startled Nomad, Sally took up the scare, and the two of them left you stranded?"

"Exactly," nodded Chris Boliver. "Still, it could have been worse, we could have had to walk right back." They were now getting into the car.

"And we could have frozen had Chris not had a jacket," came in Verity unthinkingly.

Chris finished, "And that jacket not been large enough to lend Verity one of the sleeves. I tell you my outsize tent saved our lives, or at least our comfort, last night."

"Closer settlement, no doubt," Bart said quite pleasantly, no undertone at all.

"Very close," laughed Chris. "Ever shared a jacket?"

"No. I must do it some time." Bart still kept up the mild amiability, he still did not look at Verity.

Gunnar backed the car, and they set off for the farm.

Chris was persuaded to continue on to the homestead for lunch. "And to tell Grete all about your adventure," added Gunnar with a laugh. "You know our Grete and her enthusiasms."

Verity, who had left some of her things at Chris's bungalow and would have been better pleased for them to remain there until later than have attracted more attention, heard Chris say, "But we must call first at the villa, Verity has belongings to pick up from yesterday."

She need not have concerned herself, Bart remained as supremely untouched, even uninterested. He did show interest in the cotton as they passed it, though, and the conversation . . . thankfully for Verity . . . changed focus.

The boys took over at the meal, proudly showing "Uncle Bart" how well they could speak now. Not just howareyoumate as learned from the hands as before, pointed out Ulf, but Big Words. He demonstrated, losing much of the effect by putting his Big Words in the wrong place. However, like his mother, Ulf was a cheerful person and did not mind the resultant laughter.

Much as she would have liked to have slipped away, Verity was included in Grete's furniture showing to Bart during the afternoon. Chris had gone, but not before he had arranged with Bart to view the cotton the following morning.

"Yes, I would like to see it," Bart had accepted at once, "I would like to find out the prospects of it. That's very important, I think." For the first time a look was flicked at Verity.

"The prospects are excellent," Chris assured him enthusiastically.

"Then excellent," said Bart. Although he did not look at her a second time, Verity still had a sense of being in his deliberate line of vision. It was not a comfortable feeling.

In the lumber room afterwards he accepted every piece that Grete offered. His price must have been very satisfactory, for Grete protested once: "You are too generous."

"My dear Grete, the last thing in the world I am is a benefactor, but I would never rest another moment if I was not fair." — Once again Verity had the impression of his estimating eyes on her, and yet his back was turned.

Grete went out to bring in a small piece she had forgotten, and Verity stiffened herself for the words she knew he would now say to her. A few minutes went by in silence, they seemed an eternity, then he remarked: "Quite an interesting line to that chiffonier, don't you think?"

"Bart —" If he wouldn't begin it, she must; she could not go on any longer like this.

"Also, the divan head is rather unique." Then, without drawing a breath: "Not until I see the cotton, please, see how you'll be placed."

"Placed?"

"That's what I said. You must have heard me tell Grete that I would never rest if I wasn't fair."

"What do you mean, Bart?"

"Oh, come!" he said impatiently, his head inclined to the corridor along which Grete should return at any moment. "I am well-placed ... extremely well-placed. Do you think I would let my" ... a deliberate pause ... "wife suffer with less than she could have snared?"

She realized what he was thinking. He had gathered the impression that she and Chris, that they —

"You're making a mistake, Bart," she said it urgently.

"I made it," he corrected coolly.

"Bart —"

"I made it ... but I am prepared to pay for it. Hence the cotton inspection to assess the position. No" ... as she went to speak again ... "there's nothing to be said that wasn't said in your two faces as you came along the track. But not to worry, I'll see you don't lose."

Indignation rose in Verity. "I would think you were being very magnaminous assuring that," she flung, "if I didn't know how important it all is to you." How important to get your release, she was thinking, a release without tears if possible, as it should be possible with your added money, if it's needed, to help it along. A release to go to Adele.

"Yes, it is important to me." He turned and looked at her

fully for the first time. "It's the most important thing in my life."

"Then why —" Why, she had been going to ask, didn't you wait for Robbie to die, for Adele to be free, why did you put us through all this?

"Grete is coming," he said, and his voice was cold.

The next day he spent over with Chris, then when he returned in the late afternoon she saw that his bag was in the hall and that Gunnar had the car out to take him to the airfield.

"Priscilla will be arriving," he said as he stood waiting for Grete and the boys to come and say goodbye.

"Priscilla." Verity said the name blankly, her attention elsewhere.

"She always does the after stuff." It was not a reminder of what she should know but a statement as to a stranger.

"Yes, of course," she murmured.

A short silence.

"I think you need have no fears," he said. "You know what I mean."

"I don't, Bart."

She might just as well not have spoken. "If you do have," he went on, "you know the address. However, I found that cotton very safe."

"Bart —" she began.

"Though if you believe you're not doing as well as you might have —"

"Bart. Bart, please."

He did not turn to her, but he did ask tersely, "Yes?"

"I'm sorry. It was abominable of me."

Now he must speak at last, she thought. He would agree, and she would tell him *why* she had left with only a few written words, tell him half of the fault had been his, that his voice when it had answered ... so soon ... from Adele's apartment that evening had been the real reason she had gone away. Tell him of moments when she had stood beside him in the church. Tell him ...

But what was she thinking of? This man was only interested in assuring himself that he was strictly fair and just. And only concerned for Adele.

"I'm sorry," she mumbled again.

"Not to worry." He had advised that before. He said again as he had said yesterday: "Grete is coming."

Within minutes he had left.

The week that followed prior to Priscilla's arrival to do the after-sale things was a very long one for Verity.

Chris, in his new acceptance, did not notice any difference in the girl, but sharp Grete did.

"You are not happy, Verity. It did not work out as I hoped. And yet in the beginning you two seemed to get on so well."

"What two?" For a moment Verity forgot what Grete had planned, what Chris himself almost believed he had wanted.

"You and Chris," said Grete, sharper than ever. "Who else?"

"Oh, Grete dear, it was never like that at all, and it never could have been."

"Yet Chris seems more contented," went on Grete, puzzled.

"He is, because he was one of the few who did not need your help, any of our help," said Verity gently. "For a while he believed what you urged, Grete, but it was only a phase. He is still married to that girl who died, you know."

Grete thought that over for a few minutes, then gave a little defeated smile. "Well, perhaps you are right, perhaps Chris is right."

"We are. We are sure of it."

Now Grete nodded soberly. "Yes, and I must believe it, seeing his serene face. But you, Verity, you look –" But at a look now in Verity's eyes, Grete simply touched her hand, then changed the subject.

Several days afterwards Priscilla flew in.

It seemed a lifetime since Verity had watched Priscilla go through her "after-ing" processes, the cataloguing, the recording, the describing for identification, all the necessary details that the girl did so efficiently, a lifetime away, and yet it was only a few weeks. So much had happened in those weeks. Robbie had died. She had been married. She had run away from the marriage and come here. She had met Chris, and her husband ... for a moment Verity stopped, surprised at herself, it was the first time she had said that ... and Bart had thought that she and Chris ...

"There, I think that's all for that section." Priscilla turned a page of her book.

There was something different about the girl, Verity thought, coming out of her introspection. Priscilla, as Grete had remarked of Chris, looked more at peace with herself. In fact, she looked almost –

"I suppose," Priscilla smiled, "Bart supplied you with all the Prince news."

It was Verity's turn to smile back, but it was a thin little smile, for she was thinking how meagrely Bart had spoken about anything. She heard herself murmuring, "Not expansively. You know men."

"I don't," admitted Priscilla, but she did not look wistful about it as she used to look.

"As you would know, Matthew and Cassandra are married," she told Verity, "they have a flat above Matthew's surgery. They're both rapturous – that's the only way I could put it." Priscilla looked very pleased herself, and Verity recalled her saying once that Cassandra's beauty was something she felt she could never handle.

"So," Priscilla finished, "the first of the Princes is accounted for."

Now Verity darted a quick look at the secretary. So Priscilla still did not know. Well . . . bitterly . . . that made for belief, Bart had not had time to let anyone know *before,* then *after,* with Robbie not standing between anyone any more, it had been the last thing he would have wanted to be known.

She watched Priscilla now recording the chiffonier. Was the girl's new assurance based on the welcome fact that Cassandra had been removed from the scene . . . as regarded Bart? Poor Cilla, if that was the case . . .

"How about Peter?" she inquired automatically, concluding that it was expected of her . . . then was shaken out of her polite interest by the almost dramatic change on Priscilla's face. There was no mistaking that change . . . that very lovely change.

"Why, Cilla!" she said, caught up by the girl's cheeks that had flushed to a warm pink.

As she did not answer, Verity crossed to her and tilted her chin. "Cilla, I don't understand," she begged.

"You mean," said Priscilla incredulously, "that you don't understand that I . . . that Peter . . . that we . . ." She paused to take a deep breath. "That I always –"

"No. No. I believed it was – Bart."

"Bart?" Now it was Priscilla's turn to look surprised.

"You were always so gentle with him."

"Could anyone be anything else with Bart?"

. . . Yes, thought Verity, *I* was. I was abominable with him. Even though he had been using me, how could I have done such an embarrasing, cruel thing?

"But you loved him," she said to Priscilla. "You always

161

loved Bart."

"Yes."

"He loved you."

"Yes ... but oh, Verity, never in the way you're thinking. How did you ever reach that conclusion?"

"He would look across at you. You would look back at him."

"Because there's something terribly close between us. If I could tell you –"

"You must tell me."

"It's Bart's story." – Priscilla had said this, Verity recalled, once before.

"You must tell me," she appealed with sudden urgency, "Prissie, you must."

For a few moments the girl hesitated, then with a little resigned gesture she sat down.

"If Bart hadn't done what he did, I wouldn't be here," she related soberly. "Bart saved my life. A thing like that leaves something, Verity, just as it should. I can never look at Bart now without remembering ... and thanking him for ever."

"Has this anything to do with his injuries?"

"Everything," Cilla replied.

"Then why is he still so bitter? What he has sustained can be surmounted, it has already been surmounted to a large degree, and at least he has the satisfaction that he achieved what he did with you." She waited ... then when Priscilla did not speak, she asked: "You did tell me he saved you, Priscilla?"

"But not the child," Cilla said quietly. "The little girl died."

There was silence in the room. Somewhere a clock chimed and the notes fell cool and clear. Then somewhere further away ... in the garden? ... small Ulf called. Ulf. Rising twelve robust years.

And a child had died.

Verity looked across to the secretary, and waited.

"We had this business call to this old suburban home that had been donated to a charity. Already a number of girl wards had been accepted, so more suitable furniture, child-suitable, I mean, was replacing the antique stuff. Bart, of course, was interested."

"But Bart," interrupted Verity, "wouldn't be in the business then, he only came after the accident." The accident, she thought, that had stopped his medical career.

"It should have been Peter," nodded Priscilla, "but Peter was suddenly somewhere else . . . that's Peter . . . so Bart, as he always did, stepped in to help.

"We were in the garden at the time, the little girl and I. Bart had gone into the house to talk to the matron.

"We shall never know how the hideous thing started, perhaps one of the children, even the little girl herself, had decided to burn up the dead leaves that the gardener had raked. Perhaps there was a spark from somewhere. An incinerator, or so." Priscilla sighed.

"Anyway, all I can recall is that all at once a child was aflame. I ran to her. Then" . . . a little shiver . . . "we were both alight."

"After that, I can't recall anything . . . but I've been told. I've been told that Bart leapt from the balcony from such a height and in such a way that he did much more than the usual damage a fall can do, yet in spite of the awful impact it must have been he still ran across and pulled me out and threw me to the ground, rolled me over to extinguish the flame . . . then he turned to the child and did the same."

"I didn't see it," Priscilla repeated. "I'd passed out, and anyway, people had run down and carried me off. I didn't see Bart's shocking injuries as he tried to save that child. The awful thing was he did save her, as he saved me, but what he did not know was the previous state of her heart, poor mite. As Matthew has tried to tell him a thousand times since, the child would never have grown to maturity, anyway. But Bart would never accept it. To him it was a failure on his part – a failure to save a child's life."

There was a long pause now.

"He was months ... a year ... in hospital. In that time he became very embittered. He gave away all thoughts of continuing his career. I think" ... looking at Verity ... "that that's why you coupled us. I visited Bart all the time, I understood what he was going through, because of what had happened. When two people are involved like that, there is, there has to be, an intrinsic understanding."

"Mrs. Prince also coupled you," said Verity absently. Her mind was on Bart and the horror he had known.

"I suppose so. There are things between us and I expect they must show." She looked directly at Verity. "Will you mind?"

"Mind? *I* mind?"

"Because," went on Priscilla, not heeding her, "it will always be that way ... a look and a memory. You mustn't think that –"

"*Priscilla!*" Verity waited for Priscilla to come out of herself, then she demanded: "If it was not Bart with you, then –"

"Then who?" broke in Priscilla. "But I've just told you. The other Prince, of course."

"But that leaves –"

"Peter? Yes. Then – Peter. Are you astonished? Yes, I suppose you must be. Peter has everything, I am a dull mouse."

"You're not. You never have been."

"So," said Priscilla softly, "Peter told me ... just before I
164

flew down. Verity ... oh, Verity, we're being married. I've always known for myself, and I've always sensed ... I suppose I'm being boastful ... that Peter would know, too, one day. He had to go through the gamut, he had to grow up. But he knew he was the type who needed tying ... there are people like that, you know ... and that I was the one to do it."

"A kind of mooring, Priscilla?"

"You understand it perfectly. So long as I have known the Princes, Verity, Peter has always been the 'scrape' one. As I said, he never grew up. Too much charm, too much of what it takes.

"But I knew one day he would need *me,* and when he came up from Melbourne to Sydney for Matthew's and Cassandra's wedding, it was That Day. He didn't need you, he didn't need any of the many women he had 'fallen in love with' " ... a little loving laugh ... "but old Prissie he did need. And," finished Priscilla, "I was there waiting for him."

She leaned forward to Verity. "I've sometimes wondered whether it would happen, whether it could happen, but always there persisted that feeling that it was going to happen, that it was going to be all right. Bart was aware of my feeling. He supported me. Each time he smiled at me he was telling me so ... and you thought –"

"Yes," said Verity, "I thought that."

"I'll be a restraint on Peter," admitted Priscilla, "but I think the youngest Prince has come to the stage when he's ready for that. Perhaps Peter is weak ... in fact I know he's weak ... but the weakness will pass, and even if it doesn't, I have the strength and capacity for both of us. And I feel that in time he won't resent that strength ... that he'll come to like me for it."

"He'll love you for it," said Verity, touched.

Now Priscilla's warm pink had deepened to a glowing rose.

"I know," she said softly. Then she smiled. "Because he's told me already."

A few minutes went by in happy silence.

"Another Prince accounted for," Verity said presently in a light tone.

"Yes. Only Bart to go."

Only Bart to go. If Priscilla knew the truth! Yet what was the truth? It was this: *Bart was less than married because he had a marriage that was not a marriage at all.*

"Priscilla," she broke in abruptly, "were you surprised when I went away?"

"No," answered Priscilla, surprised herself, "your brother had died, and after that you came down here for Bart. It was part of the job."

"Yes," said Verity dully, "part of the job." Then she said, finding every syllable hard but making herself say it: "Do you know that soon there'll be three Princes accounted for?"

"What do you mean, Verity?" There was a smile in Priscilla's voice, but Verity quickly stopped it.

"Bart – and my brother's wife," she said in a tight voice.

"Adele?"

"Yes. Adele."

"But you're so wrong." Priscilla was looking at her in amazement. "Never Adele," she refused.

"Always Adele ... In fact it would have happened before had Adele not lost her head when Robbie came out here."

"It would never have happened, not in a lifetime. I should know, Verity, I've been around the Princes for years. I don't say if Adele had had her way it wouldn't have come about, but never, never Bart."

"You know very little, then. You wouldn't know that Bart – that he –" But Verity's voice trailed off. How could she say to Priscilla: "You wouldn't know that my husband of only two

166

days rang Adele as soon as he knew she was free, and that he
. . . that she . . . that they . . ."

"I know a lot," Priscilla was saying confidently. "I know,
and I'm going to tell it to you, Verity, whether you are ready
for it, or not. And this is it: It's you whom Bart wants, and
has wanted right from the start. No, don't try to stop me. I've
gone through too much with Bart not to know that."

"But he never said anything."

"Bart couldn't. He was still too choked up with what had
happened to his life. He was still uncertain of himself. He
would have told you all this . . . had you helped."

Had she helped? Verity knew she had done everything –
save help.

"But Adele –" she persisted wretchedly.

"Was never anything . . . except that perhaps he was sorry
for the girl. She brought a lot of trouble on herself one way
and another, and because Bart understood trouble . . . who
would more? . . . he was always there to help a lame dog."

"He kept on helping," said Verity bitterly.

"He's a rich man."

"Not just that way." No, Verity was thinking, not just with
money but with his presence that afternoon of Robbie's funeral. An afternoon that had run into a night? Into days?
Weeks?

But it was the day of Robin . . . two days after a marriage
. . . that comprised the sharp hurt.

"But mostly that way, mostly money," Priscilla was saying
in her practical secretary way. "For instance on the occasion
of your brother's death he went over to her apartment to hand
Adele a cheque for –" She named an amount that fairly
shocked Verity into a long, long silence.

"That much," she said at last.

"That much," Priscilla nodded.

167

"Are you sure?"

"I went with him. I made it out for him. Knowing Bart as I do, I suppose I must have looked astounded at it, for he said, 'It's to be for a long time, Cilla.' He might have meant a long time for Adele . . . or he might have meant a long time for him to make out any more. For, of course, he'll be out of it all for some months."

At first her words did not sink into Verity, then slowly, starkly, they did.

"How do you mean, Priscilla?" she asked.

"Bart is going into hospital. Didn't he say? It won't be like the other clinic stays, just brief ones, it will be much more than exploratory this time. It will be the real thing. Matthew has finally persuaded Bart to go through with it, and it will mean being totally invalided for a very long time."

"When?" Verity knew it must be she who asked it, but she was not aware of opening her mouth, of making any sound.

"The first of the operations, and the indicative one, for if it is not a success, then . . ." Priscilla paused to make a little movement with her shoulders.

"Yes? *Yes*, Cilla?"

"Should be very soon. It might even be now. – Why, Verity . . . Verity, what are you doing?"

For Verity was running through the house like a whirlwind, she was calling, "Grete . . . Grete dear, I'm so sorry!

"Grete, I'm going down to Sydney with Priscilla. One day I'll come back and finish off the boys with their howareyoumate." She gave a breathless little laugh that ended in a half sob. "At least, Grete," she promised, "I'll come back to explain."

"Do you know what," said Grete who had appeared from the kitchen, "I might have been wrong about Chris, but I don't feel I'm wrong about something else. And it is this: You won't be back, Verity."

"I will, Grete. I promise."

"No, Verity, you – and Bart will be back," smiled Grete.

"Oh, Grete," Verity said, not pausing to wonder how the Swedish woman had guessed that, "please hope it. Please hope it." She added : 'Hope for us."

She was still crying "Please hope it for us", but to herself, as she threw her things into her bag.

CHAPTER XII

PRISCILLA asked no questions. She must have been curious about that mad whirlwind race through the house, the announcement that there would be two of them returning to Sydney, but when Verity came out carrying her bags, telling her that if she was finished they could leave today, that Gunnar was on the telephone now confirming their tickets, she simply, and typically, welcomed a travelling companion home.

The secretary must actually have said "home", for at once Verity was thinking: Home? But where is home? – Her Balmain flat was relinquished now, and even if Bart had not closed his own apartment to enter the hospital, could she – could she –

Oh, no, she knew, I'm not entitled.

"And I really mean home. My home." Verity's doubts must have conveyed themselves to Priscilla. "You would have cancelled your own place when you went to the Dahlquists, so now you must come with me until you start your own flatting again. That is . . . if you do." A careful smile.

Verity let that pass in her relief to have somewhere to go – and yet in an equal anxiety not to intrude now on Priscilla and Peter.

"I would appreciate it for several days, Priscilla," she admitted.

"For as long as you like?"

"And – Peter likes?" Verity smiled.

"Don't worry about that." Priscilla's rejoinder was shy but assured. "After waiting so long for Peter, it will do him good to wait for me."

"Then if you're certain –"

"Verity, I've never been more certain in my life." A pause. "Of everything. Otherwise would I be talking so confidently like this?"

"No, Pris, you wouldn't," Verity smiled back.

They had relapsed into silence, Priscilla to her dreams, Verity to her less than dreams.

The Dahlquists, Big Gunnar, Grete, Gunnar and Ulf, had come to wave them off. Just as the country plane had started along the narrow strip between the bleached grass and last year's dandelion, Chris had raced up in his Rover. Verity's final wave had been for Chris.

She looked down now at the country over which they were flying. The western plains had given way to tablelands, soon they would cross the mountains, cross the lodge on those mountains where she and Bart had spent the first night of their honeymoon . . . honeymoon? . . . one month and an eternity ago.

Then they would cover Sydney's suburban sprawl.

She dared not mull over the mess she had made of everything, and even if she had tried to do so her concern for Bart would have pushed it aside. Let him be all right, that was all she could think. Let this big, initial, indicative operation show what other operations can avail. Most of all, let Bart realize this, and persist. For, although she knew nothing of medicine, Verity was sharply conscious that half of the battle was to be Bart's, and that if he didn't offer his bit, then it would be of little use.

"Fasten up," prompted Priscilla at her side. "We're nearly there, Verity."

Verity snapped her seat belt catch, and their plane touched down.

On Priscilla's decision they went first to her flat.

"You can settle yourself in, Verity," she said. "The hospital may not want visitors around for some time yet. It will be better, anyway, to ring first."

"Yes, Pris." Verity felt she had to agree.

As they took a taxi to Priscilla's suburb, Verity repeated, "Pris, you are sure?"

"About staying with me? Very sure."

But Peter, in the flat waiting for his Priscilla, was not sure, and it was the most welcome thing, Verity told him frankly, that she had heard.

"You'll be hearing much more welcome things," Peter grinned, "but not from me. No, I'm not sure I want you here, Verity, in fact I'll be honest and assure you I don't. How long do you intend to interrupt my new love life? I don't mind a day or so, but –"

"Peter!" reproved Priscilla.

"Sorry, sweet." Peter flashed a smile at her.

As she went out to make coffee, he looked boyishly at Verity.

"When I said my new love life, I was wrong, you know, for, Verity, I think I've loved Prissie ever since I first saw her, which is a long time ago now. But I was completely self-absorbed, I wouldn't read any other signs but ones to do with me. Thank heaven Pris had the maturity to wait for me to come to my senses. I really have come to them, and all I regret now is that I never came earlier. Mad, isn't it?"

"It was mad of you, Pete," Verity replied.

He nodded whimsically. "Yet sweet, too, in a way," he went on. "There's something to be said for a late start. I know all that I'm saying now must sound pretty impossible to you, I

172

mean after you and I . . . after we . . ."

"Go on, Peter," Verity encouraged with a smile.

"Then Cassie so soon afterwards. Girls before that. Girls before that again. But –"

"But?"

"But they were nothing. You" . . . apologetically . . . "were nothing. Cass was nothing – the rest. Only one ever stood out. I think I must have known it, but wouldn't accept it. I wanted life first, or what I thought was life." He gave a comical shrug.

"But Prissie *is* my life. She's my heart, Verity, and a man can't live without his heart. – I say now, there's a pretty speech if you like," he grinned.

After a pause, he went on again. "Don't think, either, that this is another Peter-phase. It's true. It's lasting. I've had my fling, and in more ways than one. For instance, I'll definitely take over the Castle. And don't think I'm being heroic about that, I'll be taking it over because I want to. I mean that, Verity."

"Then good for you . . . but what about Bart? What about his role in the business?"

Peter smiled across at her. "Bart will never come back to it, of course."

"You mean . . ." Peter could mean several things. For instance he could mean –

"No, nothing dramatic, Verity. It's simply that Bart never did attach himself to it. Sawbones were always in his veins. – I say, that isn't so good, is it? If I'm to handle the Castle's publicity I'll have to read up on metaphors."

"Oh, Peter!" she laughed.

"No, Bart never wanted business, not really, and after he's better –"

"But will he be better, Peter? I mean – properly better? Career better?"

173

"It's more likely than unlikely," cheered Peter. "If this first go is a success, then I think there'll be nothing to stop old Bart from finishing those years he began. That is, nothing except the lack of incentive."

"Yes," murmured Verity, "incentive." She looked directly at Peter. "Why did you think he might lack that?"

"Matthew wasn't sure at any time," admitted Peter. "There's a purposelessness about Bart, Matt says. – I say that's quite a word. Purposelessness."

"Peter" ... Verity said jerkily ... "I don't think I want to hear your words. I just want –"

"Coffee? Here it is now." Peter got up to take a tray from Priscilla.

But Verity knew she could drink no coffee, not until –

"No," she said, "I just want to see Bart."

Once she had spoken she felt much better.

She was aware that Peter and Priscilla were exchanging glances, that they were glancing back at her.

Then, at a nod from Priscilla, Peter said: "I don't know if you can, but, anyway, we'll try. Come on, old girl."

By the time they reached the hospital it was to learn that Bart's first operation had been successfully concluded. – Though Matthew's face as he told them this was not as pleased as it should have been.

"What is it?" Peter asked bluntly at once.

"He's not co-operating. Even this early that is quite apparent. He's not pulling out as he should. Surgically speaking, everything has gone off perfectly. According to text, he has come through A.1. But the fact remains –"

"That he still hasn't." It was Peter again.

"No," said Matthew gravely. "He's simply lying there. And don't think that because physically he's been passed as all right he can *not* be all right. Things can still happen. Even in suc-

174

cessful cases like this, things sometimes do. In fact unless something turns the tide, he could –"

Matthew grew silent.

"All this is strictly unprofessional," he went on presently, "it is also between this family." – Family? wondered Verity, what family? But she did not wonder long in the impact of what Matthew said next.

"If Bart," he told them all, "doesn't exert himself . . . if he doesn't hold on, then –"

"Matthew." Verity's voice broke in quietly but definitely. "Can I see him, please?"

The eldest Prince looked gently at her, he even leaned over and touched her hand.

"Sorry, my dear."

"I must see him."

"He's not being seen by anyone – by that I mean anyone outside, Verity, he's not up to that stage. Why, even our mother –"

"And even his – wife?"

There was a silence. The two men looked at her, looked at each other. Priscilla looked at her. Then, without asking any questions, Matthew stood up and put out his hand to Verity.

"Come on, Mrs. Prince," he said.

Bart lay in the darkened post-op room, and one look at him told Verity *why* Matthew had spoken as he had. Bart looked frail.

"He's conscious," Matthew reported in a low voice, "but I would say barely so. He should be fully out of it by now, but it almost seems he doesn't want to be, that he's holding back on us. The thing is he *must* be out of it. Do you understand me, Verity?" He looked briefly at her. "I don't know what happened between you two, but something must have, but if you can forget it, if it should be forgotten, or remember it, if it can

175

help, then – try."

"There was nothing, Matthew" ... well, that was the truth ... "but I'll be trying." Verity sat down beside the still form.

She heard Matthew go out again, but she knew he would not go far. She knew the other doctors were waiting as well.

"Bart," she said softly, "Bart."

The man did not respond.

She sat on for a while, sat desperately. At times she repeated, "Bart –" but still he did not move. Then, unable to bear it any longer, Verity leaned over and called, "Bart, I'm here. Verity is here. Bart, your wife is here. I'm your wife," she repeated.

She said it several times more before he showed any response. Then, his eyes opening slowly, Bart Prince looked up at Verity and said: "My wife." He closed his eyes again.

Soon after, Matthew came back. Several of the doctors came with him. Verity was led outside.

It seemed an eternity before Matthew joined her, but when he came he was smiling.

"I'm not asking any questions, I'm not even asking if you went into there with a genuine reason, Mrs. Prince. No, all that can wait. Right now I'm only concerned with results."

"And they are?"

"Good. Almost miraculously so. It's remarkable how the tide has changed. He's fighting back now. Probably he'll have some tricky moments, and I have no doubt he will be a bad patient, but the thing is *he will be a patient, Verity*. He will be, my dear."

They walked along the corridor together. She asked Matthew about Cassandra, and listened, though abstractedly, to him telling her, enthusing over the newly decorated flat above the surgery, charming if not at all the grand first home he had wanted for his wife, but how Cassie adored it, how she insisted on being his receptionist-nurse, how he saw now he had been wasting his days before he married Cassandra.

"All the Princes waste their lives."

"What, Verity?"

"I'm sorry, Matthew, I was thinking of something else."

— Thinking of everything else, she could have added, than what I want to think about. "The tide has changed," Matthew had just said. "He'll be a bad patient, but the thing is he'll be a patient."

Without exactly awarding it, she was aware that he had been giving her the credit. But what did I do? she wondered dazedly. What did I say?

I want to remember . . . I must remember . . . but I still can't remember what I said to Bart.

Verity, at Priscilla's and Peter's urging, went back to Woman's Castle. She found she was glad to do so; at least the work helped fill in some of the dragging time.

She did not let herself think of the future, and she could not think of the past. It was too unhappy a past.

Bart was still in intensive care, Matthew had told Peter, and Peter had passed on to her. No visitors. No communications. Just day-by-day watchfulness. After the first tricky weeks, things should pick up.

Those weeks seemed years to Verity. When they were up, she thought, and I know, know for sure he's going to be all right, I'll step quietly out of the scene. But I'll leave an address this time, not mark it by anonymity. At least an address will be playing fair. Playing fair? She gave a little wry laugh. All's fair, she recalled, in love and war. Only as far as she and Bart had been concerned, it had been all war.

Yes, she would have to go, she continually told herself. What Priscilla said that day about Bart . . . and about me, could have been only Priscilla's imagination. It must have been her imagination, for certainly Bart had never given any sign. A girl in love, as Priscilla is, Verity shrugged, naturally would imagine love in everyone. She gave a resigned little smile.

Thinking of Priscilla brought up the subject of Adele. Had the girl also imagined something there as well? It wasn't like the efficient Prince secretary to make a mistake, but in her pink cloud nine that she lived these days. It could happen.

As though in answer to this, Adele turned up one afternoon. She was perfectly chic and very lovely, and no doubt well aware of this.

But she was a different Adele, though it took some time for Verity to believe it. Adele waited while Verity attended a customer, then she came straight to the point.

"I know you adored Robbie, Verity, and I was quite fond of him, too, in a way, so I feel I must tell you this myself, not let you hear it from someone else, and . . . well, be hurt."

For a moment Verity's heart pained her so much she felt she could not bear it. Could it be – No, Priscilla had said . . . Then Peter and Matthew had not reported . . . Besides, Bart was still not to be communicated with, so he could not have sent for Adele, have agreed with her that they –

She was not aware that in her agitation she had said Bart's name until Adele came in with a low laugh: "Oh, you're wrong to the ends of the earth there, my dear."

"But you – well, you –"

"Oh, yes, I know I let you gather that impression, it's this streak in me, I guess. I didn't have a very good time. I told you once."

"Unrewarding was your word."

"Yes, Karl was anything but rewarding." Another laugh, rueful this time.

"Karl?"

"The man I always loved but didn't get around to marry ... at least *he* didn't get around to marrying me. I wasted my best years on that fraud." A fond pout.

"I always thought you meant –"

"Yes, and I intended you to. I'm one of those mean people who have to distribute pain in the idea that it helps them with their own pain. I could never bear anyone else's happiness."

"Then Bart was never in it?"

"Only to the extent of a helping hand. That's always been Bart Prince. Incidentally, you can tell him from me that I now know the truth ... it doesn't matter how ... the truth that there's no Ramsay money, and that he came forward instead." A pause. "That's love if you like."

"For you?"

Adele stared incredulously at Verity for a long moment. "Oh, you little fool," she said at last. She waited a while, then went on. "You can tell him, too, I won't need any more handouts on your behalf. You see, Karl ..." She glanced significantly down at her hand, and Verity saw that Robbie's wedding ring had been removed ... poor Robbie ... and that another ring, a very showy diamond, now glittered there instead.

"Karl," affirmed Adele proudly. "Sometimes it's like that. Some people take a long time to come good. Karl did. And because he has, I have, too, Verity."

She was quiet for a while.

"I know what you're feeling about me, and I don't blame you, but believe me, if Robbie had to die, as he did, I made him happier than he would have been had I not come into his life. Can you at least think of it like that?"

"I'll try, Adele."

"Also, if I had been Robbie and if Robbie stood where I stand now, he would be doing what I'll be doing ... marrying again. You see" . . . a reminding little smile . . . "we were one of a kind."

"But something else has come into my way of looking at things. It's being really happy for the very first time, I expect . . . for I want to clear things up before I go off."

"With Karl?"

"Yes." A shrug. "He has a bit of clearing up to do himself. But I want you to know, and to tell Bart, that I won't ever be asking for another handout. Anyway" . . . proudly . . . "Karl has more than enough for both of us. He's certainly got himself up in the world in those years between." A smile now for Karl's success.

"Also, I want you to understand that there was nothing ever between us, between Bart and me. I looked all the Princes over years ago, having heard of their possibilities, and having managed a contact, but saw that as far as they were concerned that that was all they would ever do to me, look me over, then let it stop at that, so I concentrated instead on the soft touch of the family. Bart, of course. You'll have to watch your man with that soft heart of his."

"Bart soft?" Verity exclaimed.

"None softer."

"My man!"

"Oh, for heaven's sake, girl! Anyway, that's what I wanted to say. Also" . . . a careful pause . . . "so sorry. If you can ever find it in you to forgive –"

"Of course I can, Adele."

"And forgive for Robbie, too?"

"I think," said Verity slowly, "perhaps I should thank you for Robbie."

"Do you know what," Adele said eagerly, "that's the nicest thing you could have said."

Then she did what she had never done before, she came and kissed Verity.

Verity, watching her go, found that she was liking her more than she ever would have thought possible ... that she was waving her good luck.

Bart was out of intensive care now, and certain selected restricted visitors were being permitted. Peter and Priscilla had gone on several occasions. Cassandra. Mrs. Prince was flying back from Canada and would be seeing her son next week. Grete had rung from Tetaparilly to say she was coming down to see her antiques man. – "For the first time," Priscilla had smilingly reported Grete confiding over the long distance, "I won't be concerned about mahogany or oak."

Priscilla also told Verity that Grete Dahlquist had told her that a Mr. Chris Boliver would be calling at the Castle.

"Chris," Verity nodded.

Priscilla and Peter were again hospital-visiting the day that Chris came to the shop, but then they went every afternoon now. Verity never attended, nor had she been asked to. She knew they were all waiting for her to follow up that "Mrs. Prince" of hers, that "wife to Bart", that until she did, they were too sensitive ... for her ... to broach the subject, to tell her to come. But how could she unless Bart broached it first?

When Chris came in she was so pleased to see him, she fairly raced across.

"Hi, what's this?" he laughed. "Not changed your mind?"

"No, Chris. Changed yours?"

He shook his head. "I'm going back to America, Verity. What you said to me that night on the Outcrop put everything right for me again. I can go home, face up."

"I'm sorry you're leaving, Chris dear, yet I'm glad at the same time for you. For home is home always." She was

181

thoughtful a moment. "What about your cotton?"

"I've handed it as it is to Big Gunnar and Grete for their boys. My boys, too – I'll never have any family, Verity, so they can be my sons. Until young Gunnar and Ulf are old enough to handle the cotton, it can pay for their education at some good boarding school. Because" . . . a smile down at Verity . . . "I don't think you'll be back there, and those two imps have to learn something more than –"

"Howareyoumate. But, Chris, I could be going back."

"I'll never believe that, my dear."

He left soon after. He had a plane to catch.

"A plane," he said finally and happily, "to Elvie."

. . . Again Verity found herself waving someone good luck.

There was to be a third.

Matthew told her so the next day. Not actually a waving of luck, perhaps, but if possible a prod along the path to well-being. To achieve this for Bart . . . Bart, of course, it was, Matthew nodded . . . the doctor asked Verity to go with Peter and Priscilla on their next hospital visit.

"Remember how I said Bart would be a bad patient but that he would be a patient? Well, both have come true."

"Bart is a bad one?"

"A disappointing, even dismaying one. In short he's not progressing as he should. You did the trick last time, V, so do it again."

"Nonsense, Matthew, it was your medical know-how that achieved that. However" . . . at a shake of Matthew's head . . . "being capable of performing miracles is rather a flattering thought."

"It still wasn't medicine," Matthew persisted stubbornly. "It was you. You know" . . . quizzically . . . "you've *still* never said whether you were speaking the truth when you got your-

182

self in as you did to see old Bart, and I'm still not asking you, but I am asking you . . .appealing to you . . . to see him again."

"I can't," Verity refused. "Any move now must come from him."

"Lying prone in hospital? Unable to move? Don't be unfair, girl. Oh, no, V, it must come once again from you."

"But why? *Why*, Matthew? He is doing well. You have said so."

"But not sufficiently well. Oh, he'll recover all right, we have no fears about that, but to what degree of recovery? Verity, you did something before, so repeat the trick."

"I don't know what I did," Verity honestly replied, for she still could not remember that day clearly, it was still a daze.

But she did eventually agree to visit Bart with Priscilla and Peter.

CHAPTER XIII

Verity's heart was beating almost to suffocation as she followed Peter and Priscilla down the corridor to the room where Bart was now established . . . and would remain for many months . . . the next week-end. Stubbornly, she had refused to go until then, making her excuse an unattended shop, knowing inwardly she had to have a breathing space, a time to prepare.

"Not unattended. We'll close it," they had chorused.

"Quite unnecessary when we're so close to Saturday."

"You're a funny one, Verity."

No, Verity could have said, just an uncertain one, uncertain of what's going to happen there.

She kept well behind the pair; she did not know whether Bart had been told to expect her, and for quite a while she could not bring herself to glance up to read his reaction. By then, his surprise, if any, was over. He simply sat up, propped with pillows, looking fairly fit, if too pale and too thin.

"Once the initial awful impact of me is over, you become quite used to the sight," he tossed carelessly to Verity. That was his only greeting to her. – So Bart had regained his old astringent self.

They all talked together, Verity offering nothing to the conversation . . . until suddenly she realized that Peter and Priscilla had slipped out. That only she stood there.

"So you're back at the Castle?" Bart at length broke the awkward silence that had descended.

"Yes. That is until Peter and Priscilla . . . until they . . ."

184

"They'll probably need you even more then – keep in mind my dear parent's strong grand-maternal urge," he laughed shortly.

"I don't know if I'd stay," she told him.

"Back to Tetaparilly?"

"No."

"Then" ... with a show of impatience ... "the adjoining cotton field, seeing you like to be explicit."

"No. How could I when –"

"Yes?" he asked sharply.

"I couldn't," was all she returned.

There was another silence. Verity broke it with: "I never dreamed at any time it was – Peter and Priscilla."

"But I told you all along that Peter was accounted for."

"Perhaps ... but I still thought, at first, anyway, it was Prissie – and you."

He shrugged. "Probably my mother started the idea."

"And the glances you used to give Priscilla helped the idea along." Verity was not looking at him. "Bart" ... she said sensitively ... "I just want you to know that I've learned all about it ... I just want to say I'm sorry for what you must have gone through that time ... how you must have felt."

A look of remembered pain flicked across his face, but he managed a shrug. "I expect to a doctor, though I wasn't up to that I admit, a first death is always something that's never forgotten ... especially when it's a child."

Another silence.

Verity broke it determinedly; she felt she could not bear these pauses.

"Matthew says this first indicative operation has been completely successful, that it augurs well for any that will follow."

"Yes," said Bart, but carelessly, almost indifferently, "I, too, have been told that."

185

"Then afterwards," followed up Verity flippantly, for suddenly she was afraid of seriousness, "you'll be able to reach your heart's desire. If your brother Peter was here now he'd say 'That's a pretty speech.' " Her laugh was insincere.

She saw that he was not listening to anything Peter might say . . . only listening to what she had said.

"My heart's desire was never that," he corrected her. "Besides" . . . aimlessly . . . "I don't know if I want medicine now."

"But Peter wants the Castle."

"And will undoubtedly make a much better go of it than I did."

"I wouldn't agree." Her defence was spontaneous. "Look at your lamp collection."

"And why should I look? Not one of those lamps ever shed any light for me."

"Light?"

"Lit up one moment of truth." He was quiet a moment, but, and she saw it and repressed a little shiver, quite angrily, almost furiously so.

"Oh, for heaven's sake, Verity," he burst out at last, "let's stop patting balls at each other."

"What do you mean?"

"Truth is your name, isn't it? Then why can't you deal with that commodity, practise it just this once?"

"What do you mean?" she asked again.

"Why did you cancel out? Oh, I know you have a talent for cancelling – first Peter, then Matt, Chris Boliver after me. But why . . . *why* did you leave like that? Five words on a sheet of paper. Why?"

She did not speak.

"I hadn't hurried you. I wasn't going to hurry you. Yet you –"

"Yet I went," she nodded bleakly. "It was wrong of me. It was even abominable. I'm sorry – but I said all that before."

"You said it, but I didn't accept it. I don't accept it now. Why? Why did you do such a rotten thing?"

... Because I rang Adele and heard your voice, she thought: if you had told me before it could have been different ...

Aloud she said: "Because even though you had paid for me it didn't mean –"

"Stop it!" he came in.

"Well, you wanted to know."

"Stop it!"

After a while he spoke again. "Yes, I did pay for you, but I would still have waited until you had forgotten the money that came into it and only remembered the ..." His voice trailed off. He did not return to that theme. "When I found you'd left, I put it down to Robin," he told her. "I knew how close you two had been."

"It wasn't Robin."

"I could see that very clearly as you came back down that track that morning with Boliver. You had run away to find something, something that I could never give you, mean to you. You found it in Chris. That was obvious in your two faces. Well – fair enough. As you said, I had bought you, so I couldn't expect from you the same as I had to give."

He had to give? Bart? But Bart had never had anything to give but money. Oh, Priscilla had had her ideas, but Cilla –

"I should have stopped the caper earlier," he said it a little wearily. "Oh, yes, I could have, I knew where you had gone – heaven knows it was simple enough, you never even destroyed that newspaper ad. It was sheer luck, though, that I happened to be previously friendly with the Dahlquists, sheer luck that it was them whom you contacted. – Sheer luck, too, I dare to

187

suggest . . . for you . . . that Boliver lived so handy, and that he turned out so unmistakably decent and presentable. Otherwise I might have –"

"Might have what, Bart?"

He shrugged. "Thought out a different ending for you instead."

"There is no ending," she told him. She added bleakly, "Not yet."

"That I can well believe, for if nothing else you would be a very circumspect little girl. You would never, for instance, take on Boliver while still . . . on record only, of course . . . a wedded woman."

"I never took on Chris, as you put it."

"And you never," he reminded her thinly, "became that wedded woman. And because of that, have no fear for a happy ending in a very gratifying time. There's a special clause for instances like ours."

"Bart . . . Bart, stop all this!" Her voice must have risen, for he stopped.

"Whatever you believed you saw in Chris and in me –" she went on.

"I saw it."

"Was there only because we'd both just spilled out our hearts to each other. No" . . . as he went to make an obviously astringent comment . . . "let me finish, Bart. You see, it's not as you think."

He did not speak now, but his brows had lifted.

"Chris Boliver was still married to his dead young wife. For a little while he had thought differently . . . but he was wrong. So wrong," she finished, "he's gone back to America again. To Elvie." She was silent a while, remembering Chris's smiling face, still with that tug of sadness to the mouth, for

188

that would always be there, yet an acceptance as well. A serenity.

"Then I –" she went on.

"Then you?"

"That," admitted Verity uncertainly, "I didn't know ... though Chris seemed to think he did."

"Know what?" Bart's eyes were boring into hers.

"I don't know." Restlessly. "I tell you I don't know. – Oh, why are you probing me like this? Why has it to be your side all the time? Why can't I ask in my turn and be told? Ask how did you think I felt that day when I rang – and you answered?"

"Rang where? Answered what? What in heaven are you talking about, girl?"

"Rang Adele's apartment. The afternoon of Robbie's funeral. Only two days after –" But at that she stopped.

"Two days after a marriage that was not a marriage," he finished for her. He paused, his eyes narrowed now. "Couldn't that comprise your answer?"

"It could – and it did. That is – until Priscilla told me the truth. Told me about the cheque you handed Adele. Before that I thought –"

"Thought that Adele and I –?"

"Yes."

"You little fool!" Bart's voice was incredulous.

"I know now," she resumed shakily, "I know you paid her for the legacy she'll never receive ... will you put that down, too, in your little black book?"

"Don't talk like that, Verity."

"Then don't do any more buying of me," she cried.

"Why not? You bought me, didn't you? You bought me back."

189

"Bought you back?"

"From the devil, you must often have thought." A short laugh. "I was dying that day, Verity ... yes, I was actually dying. That sounds dramatic, but I knew as I lay there following the op that I was slipping out. And I would have – only you came and said it. You said it, Verity."

"Said what?"

Bart looked at her for a long moment ... a desperate, asking look ... then turned away.

But presently he turned back again, a little amused now, the old sharp Bart showing through.

"When you heard my voice from Dellie's," he baited, "was your pride badly hurt?"

"No, Bart" ... and she said it spontaneously ... "my heart." – Then she was looking at him in a caught-out surprise and Bart was looking back at her.

At once she was remembering sitting beside his darkened cot that day after the operation, staring down at him, trying to reach him, to keep him, then saying ... and she heard herself quite clearly now: "Bart, I'm here. Verity is here. Bart, your wife is here. I'm your wife."

"Why not?" she came back now. "Why not a heart, Bart? After all – I am your wife."

Along the corridor the first of the afternoon visitors were beginning to leave.

"Say that again," Bart was demanding hoarsely.

"Why not? Why not a heart –"

"No. No, Verity. Say – say the end."

The visitors were passing the half-opened door. Some glanced curiously in, but there was nothing to see. Bart was just looking across at Verity, and Verity was still struggling with words that somehow could not come.

"Say it," he said.

A nurse put her head round the door, glanced significantly at her watch, and intoned, "Time, please."

"Time doesn't matter," refused Bart when she had gone, "unless it's the present. I don't want to hear *then*, Verity, I don't want to hear *when*, I want to hear *now*. I want to hear it this moment." He waited.

"Very well." At last the drought was breaking. "Only you're getting it all, Bart. I was your wife. I am your wife. I will be – Oh, Bart –"

For either he had managed to lean over, or she had gone to him, but there was no distance between them at all.

"You do realize," he was whispering ruefully, "that between one thing and another, one therapy after another, it will be quite some time before you can really put signed, sealed and delivered to that wife, my girl?"

"You do realize," Verity was coming back, "that I don't believe it's going to be any time at all, my man."

"Time, please." The nurse was thinking that for long-term patient, or so she had been informed, the patient in fifteen looked a very short one. She particularly thought it as Verity was released at last from the patient's arms.

"You can still wriggle out," he warned her when the nurse had left again. "You spent a night at Adele's, remember. Then you deserted me the next day. There's such a thing as instant annulment for that."

"But there's still a night on the mountains to be accounted for," she smiled triumphantly back at him.

"Accounted for truthfully," he reminded her, "remember your name, Verity."

"I'd sooner," she admitted, "deal in fairytales than fact."

And as she went down the corridor, the nurse the winner at last, Verity found herself repeating those stories ... those childhood fantasies that she used to practise for Robbie, because Robbie had demanded that his tales be smoothly recited, no indecisions. – She found herself dealing with one particular story.

"... Once upon a time there were three princes, a gracious prince, a charming prince, a prince who was –"

A prince who was, who is, who always will be *my* prince. Verity stopped saying it to let her heart sing it instead. Something made her glance up to a window. Evidently Bart had persuaded the nurse – or another nurse – to wheel his bed there. He was waving to her. He was touching his hand to his lips to her.

She caught the kiss and imprisoned it.

Threw one back to him.